But I forgive you

The candymaker who was saved by grace

by Anita Weaver

Copyright © 2017 by Anita Weaver

All rights reserved. This book or any portion thereof may not be reproduced or used in any manner whatsoever without the express written permission of the publisher except for the use of brief quotations in a book review.

While Michael's journey is true, names, places and events may have been fictionalized for the sake of the story.

Printed by CreateSpace

Available from Amazon.com and other book stores

Printed in the United States of America

First Printing, 2017

ISBN-13: 978-1544944388

ISBN-10: 1544944381

Made in the USA
Lexington, KY
14 April 2017

Dedicated to my brother, Michael Capp, my first best friend and who was named after our great-grandfather.

ACKNOWLEGMENTS

I need to give a lot of credit for this book to Diana Grabau of Seize the Day Edits. She went above and beyond all my expectations and has made my words even better.

The Ram's Horn newspaper column is accredited to the Lake Forester newspaper, Lake Forest, Illinois.

All scripture quotes are either from New International Version or King James version of the Holy Bible.

The Two Roads and The Two Destinies chart is credited to Caleb J. Baker and portions of the text are directly quoted from Michael Capp's writings.

Introduction

How I Came to Write This Book

As a little girl, I remember hearing stories about my great-grandfather, Michael Capp. My older brother was named after him, but neither of us ever met him. He died more than fifteen years before I was born, but his life had an impact on many people, and the stories have been too compelling for me to ignore. The family story goes like this: "He was born into a Jewish family in Germany. He ran away from home in Hechtsheim, Germany at age fourteen, and stowed away on a ship. But his family forgave him. He married a gentile girl. But his family forgave him. He changed his name. But his family forgave him. Then he believed in Jesus as his Savior and his family did not forgive him."

I had many questions over the years. I would ask my Uncle Richard what happened to the family during WWII. He could only say that all of them were either dead or in the United States by then. I didn't understand how he could know that and I didn't really believe it, but I had no idea how to find out about them. Uncle Richard told me

that my great-aunt Jean and great-uncle Frank had both tried to talk to some of the Jewish relatives in the U.S., but were not well received.

My life continued and I didn't think about it much again until the 1990s. My husband and I had settled and raised our family in rural Cass County, Missouri. I became interested in genealogy, and more specifically, in my Jewish roots. Having been raised in a Christian family and community, I had no knowledge of the Jewish faith or its beliefs. Of course, we learned the Old Testament stories in Sunday school classes, but they were just stories. I did not see the connection between those stories and Jesus, my Lord and Savior.

While my girls were in school, I took a part-time job in a local library. I read several books that piqued my interest, both in the Jewish people during WWII and of the establishment of Israel as a country in 1948. The miracles that made it possible fascinated me. One of the most profound miracles was that I was actually interested in history. I was a good student in school, but history was my poorest subject and I nearly failed a required history class in college.

I met a gentleman (one of our regular patrons at the library) who shared some videos with me. They were the teachings of a Jewish rabbi who, through much study, came to believe that Jesus was the Messiah his people had been waiting for. The Rabbi taught about the Jewish holidays and their meanings in relation to Yeshua (Jesus). He even presented some Hebrew words and explained the richness of their meanings. I found that it made sense, and this revelation felt

wonderful. I realized that Jesus, a Jew, learned and obeyed all of the law and the prophets. I realized that my great-grandfather knew all of this, too. This was the beginning of my understanding of the connections I knew were there. I felt the Lord leading me to write Michael's story, but since most of those who knew him had died and I could not interview him, I knew it would be a challenge. And yet I continued to be drawn to the story and believed that writing it was one of the tasks I'd been called to do.

I began looking for Kapp families on genealogy websites. I sent out inquiries to those who were Jewish. I found information on one site about a book about Ruth Kapp Hartz entitled, *Your Name is Renée: Ruth Kapp Hartz's Story as a Hidden Child in Nazi-Occupied France*. Quite excited, I requested the book through the Inter-Library Loan service. It was only available, at that time, through the Philadelphia Free Public Library. I couldn't wait to see whether or not Ruth was related to me. On the third or fourth page, it mentioned Hechtsheim, Germany. I had never traveled in Europe, but I knew that Hechtsheim was a very small village near Mainz. Finding a Kapp in that village could not be just a coincidence. Before I even finished the book, I found the address for Ruth in Philadelphia and wrote her a letter. I finished reading the book about her family's experiences in WWII. In it, she told about the ways her life was spared due to the kindness of French families and of the nuns in a French convent. I knew this was the answer to the question I had asked my uncle so many years earlier. Members of our family *were* Holocaust survivors and victims. I longed to meet Ruth, but I knew that being a Christian

might be an obstacle. I made it clear in my letter that I wanted to give her the option of leaving the past behind. I told her I wouldn't contact her again unless she wanted to explore our common roots. Amazingly, on Easter Sunday morning in 1998, the phone rang. It was Ruth. She and I talked for quite a while. At one point she said, "You know, your Jesus' last supper was a Passover Seder." I said, "yes," and tears started running down my face. Her call began a friendship and healing that was generations in the making for the Kapp/Capp families. I owe a debt of gratitude to Ruth for being willing to cross that chasm that had separated our family for so long.

Ruth went to schools, churches, synagogues, and public meetings telling her story of being a "hidden child." Her speaking engagements took her all over the world, but to this day she has not come to Kansas City and I have not been to Philadelphia, so we have not met face to face. Even so, her friendship and help has been extremely valuable to me. She told me about others in our family that she had met in her travels.

In the year 2000, my brother Mike went to Germany, and Ruth put him in touch with one of her friends who was very hospitable and helped him go to the Jewish cemetery in Hechtsheim. The cemetery is locked and is only accessible through the caretaker. In the fall of 2006, I was also able to go to Germany. My daughter's husband was stationed on a military base near Kaiserslautern—only about a forty-five minute drive from Hechtsheim. Ruth's friend was traveling at that time, so she was not able to escort me to the cemetery as she had my

brother a few years earlier. I had made the acquaintance of a gentleman named Reinhard who had worked at a girl's school in Mainz. He originally contacted me concerning some Kapp family members who had attended that school. He was trying to find out what had happened to these girls after the war. Unfortunately, it was years later before I could find that information for him. He and his wife welcomed me, my daughter, and my two small grandchildren as guests in their home. He went with me to the cemetery and acted as translator. The caretaker spoke only German, and although I had taken several German classes in high school and college, it was very helpful to have Reinhard there. Reinhard and his wife continued a friendship with my daughter and her family for several years.

In December 2007, Ruth contacted me and asked me to answer the inquiries of a young man in Israel. Ruth and I had worked on a family tree and we knew we were related, but she felt I could help this young man better than she could. Due to my mother's death, it was a few weeks before I contacted T. Kapp in Israel. Communicating through the internet and by phone, we combined his family tree (the one branch of the family neither Ruth nor I knew about) with ours. It was a perfect fit. All the branches went back to Hechtsheim and Worms, Germany, in the early 1800s. We worked together for hours and now have a beautiful and complete family tree. T. carefully told me about each family member in Israel, and of his grandfather who came to Palestine from Germany. I told him all I could about his American cousins. In the fall of 2008, T. came to the United States and

visited us. He introduced me (by internet and phone) to other Kapp family members in New York. Vivian is related to T.'s father. She and I found we had a lot in common. She is my age and has daughters like I do. She loves reading, and we have recommended books to each other. I have very much enjoyed getting to know Vivian, and she has shared family information from Worms, Germany, for our family tree. T's friendship has been such a blessing to me. He even tried to teach me Hebrew, but I admit I wasn't a very good student. I still find Hebrew very difficult to read and write—much less speak. Maybe someday I'll get it, T.

Early in my research I communicated with Ruth Vance, whose grandfather was Dr. Walter Wilson. Dr. Wilson was a medical doctor and hosted a popular radio show in Kansas City during the 1920s and '30s. His wife, Marian Baker, was the daughter of Caleb Baker. Caleb Baker was one of the leaders of the group who moved from Chicago to Kansas City in 1903 to establish Central Bible Hall. He was also one of the partners in the Baker–Lockwood Tent and Awning Company. That company provided the Big Top tents for Barnum and Bailey and Ringling Brothers circuses. They also provided the tents for Michael Capp's meetings. Ruth Vance gave me lots of information about her family and Baker–Lockwood Tent and Awning Company. Ruth and her husband were missionaries to Brazil for many years, and they now live in Texas. I have appreciated all of Ruth's help.

Another person who has helped me collect information about Central Bible Hall is Ron Beard, who lives in Leavenworth, Kansas.

He supplied me with names and dates from the early years of Central Bible Hall.

In the 1990s I was given the names of Albert and Marta Shutt in Alpena, Arkansas. They sent me tracts written by my great-grandfather in the early 1900s. I remember receiving them, and in the parking lot of my daughter's school I read them for the first time. Tears ran down my face, knowing I was reading Michael Capp's own testimony about his search for peace with God and how his son's death affected his faith. The congregation at Alpena Pass, though small, still exists. The Shutts also gave me information that led me to the Lawrence London family in Henryetta, Oklahoma.

On Christmas morning of the year 2012, Albert and Marta's daughter Ruth Perkins contacted me. She sent me information about Michael from Moody Bible Institute that I had never seen before. It verified Michael's love for his people, the Jews, and his desire to share the gospel with them. I am grateful for her willingness to look up information for me in Chicago and to help put the story together.

I know there are many more places and testimonies that I have missed, and possibly will never know about, but these people have freely shared their memories and thoughts about my great-grandfather's work in their communities.

Another interesting discovery during my research involved the Frito-Lay Company. An elderly family member told me that Michael

played a role in the development of the snack called Cracker Jacks. I looked for the story of that particular confection and found the story of the Rueckheim brothers. I noticed in a city directory that they lived in the same block in Chicago where Michael lived in the 1880s. The Rueckheim's story about Cracker Jacks left room for the possibility of Michael being a part of that process. Today, the Frito-Lay Company owns Cracker Jacks, and after examining the documents, their lawyers told me that they could neither confirm nor deny that Michael was involved. They knew my motives were pure and that I was not interested in financial gain, just the truth. They said there was another name on the documents, but it had been removed.

When I was about ten years old, I remember reading a story at my grandmother's house. She had bookshelves in a corner of the front room, and my brother and I enjoyed many happy hours in that corner. The story was written in pencil on a piece of paper and tucked inside the front cover of a book. It was the story of the stripes on candy canes, the same story that became popular at Christmas time in the late 1990s. When I saw the story printed on cards and attached to candy canes, I knew I had seen that story before. I researched it and even talked to Bob's Candy Company, who makes most of the traditional candy canes sold today. As with the Cracker Jacks story, I was not able to completely prove or disprove my great-grandfather's involvement with the stripes on candy canes, but I found several key elements to the story that are consistent with Michael's life. The story always describes the candy maker as a Jewish man, that he had received Jesus as his Savior, and that he was either in Illinois or

Indiana. I don't know if Michael was ever in Indiana, but he wasn't far from the state line when he lived in Chicago. I know candy canes were made in other places as well, but the particular design of red stripes representing Jesus was first done in the late 1800s.

These stories would be consistent with the teachings of the Plymouth Brethren. They often remained anonymous, or removed their names from any worldly gain or fame. In their minds, God is to receive the glory for anything good we accomplish—not ourselves. That made it impossible to prove many of my theories, but I have come to recognize my great-grandfather's writing and make some educated guesses about his work.

Finally, I must acknowledge my family. My dear Aunt Connie, my Capp cousins, my sister and brothers, my husband and daughters. All have contributed to making this story. My daughter Laura Gray has especially been helpful getting all these words into a form that can be read either on paper or electronically. Thank you, and I hope you know how much I love you.

It has been quite a journey for me in the presenting and telling of Michael Capp's life story. I've found that his personality and adventures have become woven into my own life story. The Lord has brought wonderful people and experiences to me. I have learned more about Michael, myself, and the Lord we both love. I may never get to travel to Israel, even though it has been a desire of my heart for years. But the Lord brought T. into my life, and with him, a piece of Israel. I

may never meet Ruth Hartz face to face, but she helped me develop a deep love for G_d's chosen people that I never could have imagined. Perhaps southern Missouri and northern Arkansas would have become an environment rich with Bible-believing people anyway, but I can't help but think that my great-grandfather's work of bringing the gospel to that area was at least part of the reason that today, in Branson and the Ozark hills, the gospel of Jesus is shared freely at Silver Dollar City and the numerous music shows. Performers in the shows there, like nowhere else, talk freely about their faith in Jesus. I cannot prove for sure that my great-grandfather was at the Chicago World's Fair with the Rueckheim brothers peddling Cracker Jacks. And I cannot say with one hundred percent certainty that Michael Capp was the candy maker who added the stripes representing Jesus on candy canes. In my heart, though, I know that these things are true. I pray that as you read his story, you can get to know Michael as I have—a rebel who found Jesus and heard Him say, "But I forgive you."

Chapter One

Seeds of Rebellion

Although most of us go through a time of adjustment as we move into adulthood, it seems that some of us just don't mold into that person our parents and teachers hoped we would become. We hate the thought, and resolve to never be satisfied with that life. We disobey and disrespect our parents over and over, causing all sorts of trouble and pain to those who love us. Finally, we come to a point when the comforts of home are no longer comfortable—a time when family ties seem to be tied way too tight—and a time when the rules of family and community seem entirely too restrictive. Home seems small and confining, like a pair of shoes that we've outgrown. We refuse to be denied the excitement of exploring all that the world has to offer, so we break away, feeling angry—and yet somehow, free.

That time for me, Michael Kapp, came in the spring of 1871. I was fourteen years old, and I couldn't wait to get away from my home in Hechtsheim, Germany. My older brothers, Bernhard, Emanuel, and Siegfried, had settled into lives of either cattle dealing or fruit growing in the village located along the Rhine River. Albert, my younger brother by two years, was playful, yet studied diligently for his bar mitzvah. Our sister, Johannette, was twelve. She worked with our mother doing the daily cooking and cleaning. Vater, which is the German term for father, was one of our religious leaders. Although there were only about seventy-five people in the village, he taught from the Torah and officiated at weddings, funerals, and Brits, the Jewish rite of circumcision.

Vater, very serious and strict, did not tolerate any laziness or disobedience. I could not please him—ever. The more he demanded from me, the less I wanted to do things his way. He'd always ask, "Why can't you be more like your brothers?" and when I didn't do my lessons perfectly, he'd slap my hands with a wooden stick. My mother was often in tears because of my stubborn disobedience and pranks, but I didn't care.

Most of the people in our village were related to us. Aunts, uncles, cousins—all were either from the Kapp, Weiss, Selig, or Schlosser families. They spread the stories of my latest misdeeds, and since I was in trouble so often, the adults didn't want me around the younger children.

The leaders in our village had hired a man named Samuel Reiss to teach the children through the age of thirteen. He, like Vater, was strict and intolerant of my antics. By the time of my bar mitzvah, he was glad to be done with me. For the next year-and-a-half, I helped Siegfried in the orchard and did as little work as possible. I sat by the riverbank for hours and watched as boats went up and down the Rhine carrying cargo and passengers. "Where are they going?" I wondered. "What's around the bend in the river?" I really wanted to know. I dreamed of the day that I could find out.

I talked with my cousin Benjamin Albert about leaving. He was two years younger than me, but we both dreamed of going to America. We planned to walk to Mainz, go down to the river where the boats docked, and sneak on board when no one was watching. We both knew we could not leave during Pesach, or Passover, but as soon as the holiday was over we would make our move. Each day seemed longer than the last. The story of the Exodus from Egypt was read every day, as it always was during the eight-day festival. "Soon," I thought, "I will be free from my slavery."

Benjamin worried that someone would find out about our plans and stop us. I knew that some of the family might actually be glad when they discovered I was gone. Maybe they would have even helped me pack. I was more concerned about what would happen once we were on the boat, though. My heart raced at the thought of the adventure.

The night before our planned escape, I gathered together a change of clothes, a small amount of money, and some bread and apples and put them into a bag. I stuffed it under my bed. The plan was that I would meet Benjamin outside the village at sunrise. I was too excited to sleep, but I tried to get a little rest. We'd have plenty of time to sleep once we were on the boat, I thought.

At the first sign of light I got up from my bed, grabbed my bag, and crept out of the house. My younger brother Albert, who slept in the same room with me, rolled over but did not wake up. I knew it would only be a short time before everyone would get up to start their work. Mutter would make a breakfast, and although it was tempting to wait, I knew I needed to be gone before then.

Benjamin stood in the dim light under the tree where we had agreed to meet. He seemed nervous. "I don't know about this," he said.

"It will be fine," I told him. "You'll see after we get onboard."

"Then what?" he asked.

"Then we'll be on our way to a new life," I told him.

We walked quickly. Our legs pumped in sync, and although it didn't matter now, we both tried to keep our footfalls quiet as we headed down the road toward the river. Benjamin looked back over his shoulder from time to time. I had gone to the docks with my brothers many times to send or pick up goods. As usual, there were a lot of people. I hoped none of them would recognize Benjamin or me.

Nothing seemed unusual, but I knew today would be different. I wouldn't be going back home.

"Just act normal," I told Benjamin. "Don't let anyone suspect anything other than we are here to look over the goods."

We walked among the cargo and merchants. I looked at the different boats, sizing up which one would be easiest to board without being noticed. After awhile, I saw a boat without anyone near it. I pushed Benjamin ahead of me and squeezed behind some crates, and we stuffed our bags in the small space with us. We sat down on the deck and waited and waited. We had to stay quiet and patient. For us, that was not easy. It seemed like forever before the crew came back and the boat pushed away from the dock.

We were on our way, but to where? From our position we could not see the scenery along the river. We could only see blue sky and puffy white clouds, and feel the sun streaking down to warm us briefly from time to time. I noticed Benjamin had fallen asleep and knew this was my opportunity to rest as well, so I closed my eyes and relaxed.

When I woke, I didn't know how long it had been, but I heard voices. The sun had disappeared, and grayness surrounded us. Benjamin still slept, so I nudged him, my fingers to my lips. I could tell from the voice of authority that it was the captain of the boat talking with someone about the trip. He said there would be several stops to load or unload supplies—first at Koblenz, then Bonn, Kohn,

and finally, Dusseldorf. I had heard of these cities, but had never been so far from home. The weather was good, he said, but I could tell it was much cooler than when we left.

Benjamin whispered that he was hungry. Until then it had not occurred to me that we had not eaten anything. I took bread and an apple for each of us out of my bag and wondered how long our food would last. We ate silently. Could we stay in our hiding place overnight? Our bodies were cramped and we had no water. We had to have some relief soon. What if our hiding place was exposed when supplies were moved on or off the boat?

The boat jolted and then stopped. I assumed we were at Koblenz. The voices had gone, so I took a chance and stood up to stretch and look around. I didn't see anyone, so I motioned for Benjamin to stand up too. We walked a little, looking over the layout of the boat. We guessed that the boat was manned by only a handful of men. Before long, two of them came into view, rolling some barrels down the deck. They'd seen us. I quickly devised a plan.

"Let's ask them for a job," I whispered to Benjamin. We approached the man we thought was the captain.

"We would like to work for you," I said, "in exchange for passage to Dusseldorf."

He looked at us without speaking, and I wondered if he knew how young we were or that we had already been on his boat since

Mainz. His face looked like stone, and I couldn't tell. Maybe he was used to stowaways.

"Fine. Move those crates onto the boat," he said, pointing to some wooden boxes on the deck. Benjamin and I went right to work. It felt good to use our stiff muscles. After we finished, the captain told us to sit down on a bench. He and the crew started up the boat again and moved it out into the river channel.

We were more comfortable for the rest of the trip, but I could see that Benjamin was having painful doubts about leaving home. "I want to go back," he finally cried out.

"We can't go back now," I said, the knot in my stomach nearly as painful as his must have been.

The captain and his crew shared their food with us, but we managed to keep from telling them much about ourselves. We did what they told us and then retreated to our corner of the boat. At Dusseldorf, however, I knew we'd have to decide how to get to Bremen. We had heard that Bremen was where the big ships were that sailed to America. We docked two more times and finally arrived at Dusseldorf.

Benjamin's adventurous spirit was totally exhausted. He made it clear by his stubborn refusal to make plans that this was the end of the trip for him. He wanted to go back on one of the riverboats, but I just couldn't give up. I felt sad about Siegfried and Mutti and knew

they might be worried, so I asked Benjamin to give them the simple message that I was sorry. The captain agreed to let Benjamin work his way back to Mainz, and after giving him an awkward hug, I got off the boat and walked east. And so we parted ways. I was alone.

Several wagons filled with straw lumbered down the road and I hopped onto the back of one. Darkness enveloped us by the time the wagon pulled into a large city. Hungry and thirsty, I took a few coins and paid for a loaf of bread at a small bakery. If I was careful, I thought, it would last until I could get on a ship to America. I came upon a soft haystack, lay down, and closed my eyes.

I woke with the sun and looked around. The streets bustled with people and wagons. I walked down a street and took in all the sights and sounds. It seemed that the crowds were all flowing in one direction, so I followed. The street ended at a dock. Not like the river docks, but much bigger. I lifted my eyes and saw a huge vessel, the largest I'd ever seen. On the side were the words *Graf Bismarck*. I watched some men load cargo, lugging it up the gangplank and onto the ship.

I was determined, yet knew I must be careful not to be discovered. I didn't know what would happen if I was found without a ticket. If I had known about the *Graf Bismarck's* first voyage only a few weeks earlier, I might have changed my mind and walked back toward home, or at least chosen another ship.

Chapter Two

The Graf Bismarck

I stayed out of sight as much as possible during the ship's loading. The people kept coming in a long stream, each one straining under the weight of their bags. I lost count, but it was more than I had ever seen in one place before. The whole village of Hechtsheim contained less than one hundred people, and I had counted at least a hundred and fifty as they walked up the ramp. Some headed to the cabins—families of men, women, and children. I grieved as I thought about my family and the fact that no one would be waiting for me in New York. I would have to deal with that later. I couldn't turn back now, so I pushed down the sad feelings and refused to honor my parents by allowing myself to even think about them.

The rest of the people streamed into the lower levels of the ship. I fell into the line and followed. The lower deck consisted of a

huge area where the majority of the people situated their belongings and settled down. I followed the crew another deck down where the coal and steam engine operated, clanging and hissing. The crew's quarters were on that level along with the cargo.

The fires were stoked and the steam began to build the power needed to move the huge vessel. I felt movement and knew we were on our way. I sat behind some of the barrels in the hold of the ship and ate the end of the bread I had bought with my last coins the night before.

After a few hours I grew curious about the ship and emerged from my hiding place. Some of the crew saw me. They had to have known I was not a paying passenger. My guilt must have shown. It was hot and dirty in the lower part of the ship, and I longed for fresh air and a comfortable space to sit or lay down. I didn't know then that for the next two weeks I'd be confined to cramped quarters and would only have a few opportunities to see daylight.

The crew whispered as I walked past them, and I knew they were talking about me. They would look at me with scorn and play tricks on me. One of their favorites was to set some food out on a crate and leave it. From a distance they bet on how long it would be before I grabbed it. To me it felt like a trap for a varmint. They'd set it and I'd take the bait. After a day or two, I was so hungry that I didn't care. At least I'd have a bite of food every now and then, even if it meant I was their entertainment. Maybe it decreased my risk of being thrown off the ship. They tormented me by telling loud stories of how they put a

stowaway into a barrel and drilled him an air hole. They laughed at their prank and at the way the poor chap had cried out miserably for mercy. Just to add to their fun, they had turned the barrel upside down. I didn't know for sure if they had really done it, or were just telling the story to frighten me. No matter which it was, I was scared.

My fears multiplied as I overheard them talking about their last trip, the first time the *Graf Bismarck* had sailed to New York. She left Bremen on the twelfth of February, well-stocked and carrying only fifty-two passengers. On schedule, she touched Southampton on the fifteenth. At sea, a gale developed into a hurricane that continued without pause for thirty-six hours. It was horrible. The cabins flooded several times and the winds tossed the ship violently. Much of the crockery and merchandise was destroyed. Three days later, on February 27, another hurricane overtook her, this time with thunder and lightning. For ten hours the gale pounded the ship, with a force and violence that momentarily threatened to engulf the steamer and all on board. During six of these hours the ship refused to mind her helm, leaving her at the mercy of the wind and waves and almost drowned amid the billows. Captain Meyer said that the sea during this storm was more violent than anything he had ever seen before in the whole of his professional service. During the lull that followed this storm, the Bismarck encountered large ice fields, and a number of the icebergs were nearly one hundred feet high. These were unusually situated in an area of open ocean, where icebergs are rarely visible. After parting company with the icebergs, the *Bismarck* was enveloped in a snowstorm of fifteen hours' duration, during which it was impossible

to see the length of the ship. The snow accumulated on her decks to the depth of a foot and a half.

Each crewmember added his own account of that trip. The *Bismarck* finally arrived in New York on March 6, but many there had feared the ship had been lost at sea. Although the cargo was totally gone, no lives were lost. Some of the crew left and vowed to never board a ship again. Who could blame them? Others believed that the *Bismarck* had passed the test and was built solidly enough to survive those obstacles and any others she might encounter in the future.

On the third day our ship stopped. I wondered if we could be in America already. The crew unloaded a few crates, then brought even more onboard. I heard them say "Southampton." I gathered from their stories that we had only begun, and it would be a long time before our feet would touch ground in America.

One of the older crewmembers with a kind face came to me and said, "Come here," and pointed to a dark corner. I followed. Looking around to see if anyone else was near, he said, "Listen. When we launch again, I'll take you to steerage. You can mingle among the passengers and they'll think you boarded at Southampton. If anyone asks your occupation, say 'merchant.' Got it?" I nodded. "Maybe one of the mothers will adopt you for the rest of the trip."

As he promised, the man took me to the deck above and left me there. I saw a man and his wife with a boy about my age. I stood near them, and eventually the woman asked me my name. "Michael," I told

her. They were the Dydrink family from Schleswig-Holstein—Ludwig, Anna, and their son, Helmund. Helmund was actually a year older than me, but I didn't reveal my age. The Dydrinks were kind, and as the crewmember had said, Anna treated me very motherly. Ludwig was a workman and was going to build a house for them in America. Anna's family had come earlier and had settled in Iowa.

The steerage had many interesting characters. Some were rough looking, but most just hoped to start a new life in a new land. A young man from Switzerland named Melchior claimed to be a baker. Another from Peoria, Illinois, named Joseph, said he was a confectioner. He told us about his family's grocery store and how he made sweet treats to sell. He gave me a sample of his candy—he called it a peppermint stick. When they asked me about my profession, I answered "merchant," as the crewman had advised me. If asked, I didn't know what kind of merchandise I would say that I sold. But no one asked.

The days lingered on and on. The steerage community was getting comfortable living together. The Dydrink family always shared food with me, and I was thankful for their generosity. At night, there always seemed to be music. It was surprising how musical instruments could be made from almost anything and how the voices blended. Many hours passed in this pleasant way. I didn't know any of the songs, but I enjoyed the singing and dancing. It took me only a few days to learn some of them.

Sleeping on the boat was challenging. With so many people aboard, there always seemed to be noise. Finding a place big enough and comfortable enough to stretch out also presented a problem. I found that I had to take advantage of any opportunity to rest. Most of the time we didn't know if it was night or day. I lost track of how many days it had been since we'd left Southampton. I was pretty sure it had been five days from the time I left home until I boarded the *Bismarck*, and another three days to Southampton, but after that I couldn't tell.

Occasionally we would go to the upper deck, but there was nothing to see except water. The air in mid-spring was still a bit chilly without a coat or wrap, so we were careful to stay warm and dry. The rolling motion of the ship bothered me at first, but I finally adjusted to it. Staying below seemed easier on my stomach than being on the upper deck.

One of our main concerns was that someone would become really sick—not just seasickness, but with an actual disease and fever. Thankfully, that was never a problem.

Joseph, Melchior, Helmund and I played games and told stories. We were all about the same age. They talked about their dreams and their homes. I just listened. If they asked me questions, I avoided answering. I thought that selling candy like Joseph sounded interesting. He even offered to help me find a job if I came to Peoria. I told him I'd think about it.

One morning I woke up and realized the ship was no longer moving forward. The other people in steerage also began to realize that the ship had stopped. After a while we heard the first-class passengers moving around above, so we went up to the main deck, too. The crew on deck tied the ropes to a smaller vessel. Two people, a man and a woman, climbed aboard the ship.

They checked everyone onboard. They looked at our eyes, peered in our throats, and felt our foreheads for fever. They said they were making sure no one was sick. When they found that all on board were healthy, the ship was allowed to enter the harbor and an anchor was lowered. Shortly, barges and tugboats came alongside the *Bismarck*. We were instructed to bring our luggage and board the smaller boats in family groups. The Dydrinks, Melchior, Joseph and I stayed together and got on a tug. The short trip to the pier led to a large building called Castle Garden. It sounded like a beautiful place, but when we walked inside I saw only a mass of people. It was overwhelming.

Chapter Three

Castle Garden

Inside the huge building a multitude of loud voices made it nearly impossible to hear. It must have been like this at the tower of Babel—people speaking in many languages and trying to understand each other. It had never occurred to me that there would be people speaking different languages in America. On the ship I'd heard a few other languages, but most spoke German or English. The Dydrinks spoke German, but it sounded funny. The area of Germany where they lived was nearer to Denmark, and we called their dialect Low German. The German in Hechtsheim was High German, mixed with some Hebrew. Melchior spoke Swiss, which also sounded funny, but I could understand much of it. Joseph spoke English, but he could speak German as well, and he taught me some English words. At Castle Garden it became very clear to me that I would need to know a lot

more English to survive in America, as English was the tongue of choice.

We were checked again to confirm our health. Then we were directed to an agent who spoke German. The agent had so many questions. Did we have money to exchange? I did not, but my friends all needed to exchange theirs to American currency. Did we have family waiting for us? Anna Dydrink's family was expecting them, but had not come from Iowa to meet them. They planned to catch a train to Iowa as soon as possible. Joseph's father had come to New York and was waiting for him. Melchior's family lived in New York, and he had only to find transportation to their house. I could not answer the question. No one was here from my family.

The agent looked at my name and asked, "Are you kin to Friedrich Kapp?" I did not know. "Mr. Kapp was the immigration officer until a few months ago," the agent said.

"I do not know him," I answered. The others were directed to another line and I was told to step to the side. I knew this was where I would be on my own again, as Joseph, Melchior, and the Dydrinks moved where they were told. Anna Dydrink looked back at me and I could tell she wanted to take me with them, but I did not have papers.

The agent asked, "How old are you?"

"Vierzehn," I responded.

The agent fired the next question. "What city are you from?"

"Hechtsheim am Main," I told him.

"You wait right here," he said. I decided it was better to obey than to run, even though my heart was racing and I was tempted to burst out the closest door. I couldn't see the Dydrink family any more, and I did not know where any of the doors led or what I would encounter on the other side.

The agent and two or three others held a conference. After a minute or so, they came back. They explained that I was not sick, but the procedure was to send unaccompanied children under the age of eighteen to Ward Island. There, a matron would care for the children until parents could be located or until they were moved to an orphanage. My fears boiled inside and I didn't know what to do. Where would they send me? The agent's voice softened a little, I thought, as he brought me behind his window and gave me a chair to sit in.

"Don't worry. We have sent for the police," he said. I did not know what that meant, but it didn't sound good at all.

A few minutes later, a man in a blue suit with many gold buttons and medals on it came over to me. He spoke German. "Guten Tag," he said. "Ich kenne Captain Schultz. Bitte, kommen sie," and he pointed to an exit. Outside was a dock where we got into a small tugboat. It went back upstream. When the boat stopped at an island, Captain Schultz told me to get out. We went into a building and I saw children of all ages, but it looked like I was the oldest. Captain Schultz

told me that he wanted me to meet someone. We went to a room and he knocked on the door. We entered and another man with even more gold ornaments sat at a desk. He stood. Captain Schultz introduced me to Superintendent of Police George Walling. Since he didn't speak German well, Superintendent Walling asked Schultz to stay and interpret.

"Your name is Michael Kapp. Is that correct?" he asked.

"Ja," I replied.

"And where is your home, Michael?"

"America?" I said.

"No, I mean where do your parents live?"

"Hechtsheim, Germany."

"Okay. Do they know where you are?"

"Nein."

"So, do you know anyone with whom you could stay until we send you back?"

"Nein, nein, nein. Ich will in Amerika bleiben."

"He wants to stay here," Schultz said. A look of concern passed between the two men and I knew it wasn't going to be that easy.

Captain Schultz repeated everything the Superintendent said so that I would understand. He told me that just outside the doors were dangerous gangs of boys who had nowhere to live. They would wait along the riverfront for people who were new to this country and who might have money or possessions that they could steal. Many people had been robbed, beaten, and murdered by these thugs. And the immigrants' only mistake was being in the wrong place. A single young man like me would have no choice but to join them in their terrible deeds or be killed by them. He said, "You cannot live alone on the streets of New York. You know, one of my jobs is to protect people, especially children."

"Ich bin kein Kind." He understood from the tone in my voice that I didn't appreciate being called a child. I explained that I was a man, and had been ever since my bar mitzvah over a year earlier. I struggled to hold back the tears of fear and anger that welled up inside of me.

Schultz and Superintendent Walling talked among themselves for a while. Finally, Schultz said, "Michael, sie konnen mit mir nach Haus kommen" (You can come home with me). "Meine Frau und ich werde Sie bleiben, bis wir herausfinden, wo Ihr dauerhaftes Zuhause sein wird" (My wife and I will let you stay until we figure out where your permanent home will be). "Sie mussen hier bleiben, bis meine

Schicht vorbei ist obwohl" (You have to stay here until my shift is over, though). I decided to take his offer. We left the office and Schultz instructed the matron in charge of the children to feed me. It was so good to have something in my stomach again.

It had been a long day, and I had nothing to do but watch people. Sick people were taken to another part of the building. Family members of the sick frantically tried to find out where their loved ones had been taken and when they could see them again. Most of the time, the answers were not satisfactory. Sadness and tears filled the huge room and echoed off the walls. My situation didn't seem as hopeless any more. Even though I was alone and penniless, I was well.

When Officer Schultz returned for me, I was long past ready to go. He asked about my luggage and was shocked at my small bag. We walked out of the building and I nervously looked around, checking for the gangs. I realized that being with a police officer gave me a certain amount of security. We took a boat to the mainland and then walked up a street to a horse-drawn train. Schultz paid the fare. The train passed many buildings and houses. It stopped often and people got on and off, but Schultz remained seated. What would Frau Schultz think when her husband walked in the door with me? Would she be as kind to me as her husband had been? The dark streets and the unknown revived my fears. Finally, Schultz stood up and motioned for me to follow. The train came to a full stop and we jumped off.

The Schultz's home was only a block or so from the train stop on 111th Street. I asked Schultz if it was true that there were over a

hundred streets in New York. He laughed. "Ja," he said. I couldn't wait to see this city in the daylight.

Frau Schultz met us at the door, and two little girls hid behind her. Then they ran past their mother and into their father's arms. They hugged and giggled until the Frau told them to go and wash. After greeting her husband with a kiss and a few whispered words, Frau Schultz introduced herself as Mary, and then she introduced the girls. Young Mary was nine years old and Jennie was five. Although Frau Schultz spoke to me in German, English was the language they used and taught the girls. She had a hot meal waiting on the table. Young Mary got another plate, a fork, and a cup of water for me. I thanked her. All of us sat down. Schultz bowed his head and said some words. I did not understand what he said, but it seemed like some kind of blessing. It was definitely not a Jewish blessing, and I was sure the food was not kosher, either. It didn't matter. It was very good. I was not planning to keep the traditions from home, anyway.

After dinner, Mary and the girls cleared the table and began washing the dishes. Schultz told me to call him William. We stepped outside and talked. He wanted to know why I had left home and how I expected to make a living now. They were hard questions that I hadn't even answered for myself. I told him about my family in Hechtsheim. Raising cattle and fruit was the only experience I had. He told me I might have to learn something else to do or else move west. I told him about Joseph's offer to give me a job at his family's store in Peoria. William laughed and told me that it was a long way to Peoria. Without

money, I couldn't even get to the New York City limits. He recommended that I stay with them and get prepared for life. There were trade schools and places where I could learn English. As long as I stayed with them, William told me I would have to either go to school or to work, starting immediately. I would also be required to do chores, and if I got a job, I would have to pay rent. It sounded like a lot of rules, but William and Mary were kind, and I wanted to stay.

Chapter Four

The Letter Home

I enjoyed living with the Schultz's and being part of their family, yet sometimes it seemed awkward. Their family was much different than the one I had left, and I didn't understand why they cared about someone like me. Mary was kind, and although she expected me to help her with the daily housework, she made time each day to help me learn English. When I played games with the girls, I learned even more English words and phrases. William took me to a "schul" in the evenings to learn English and also to learn how to become a United States citizen, but the thought of schul brought back unpleasant memories, and I told William I wouldn't go. As we had agreed, William helped me look for a job. Of course, he could only do this on the days he didn't work. I was unqualified for most jobs, and it was difficult to find someone who would trust me.

A couple of weeks after William took me in, Superintendent Walling came to the Schultz home. He wanted to talk to both William and me, in private. Mary and the girls left to go to the market. Superintendent Walling handed me a paper on which some German was written. I could tell it was a letter from my Mutter. William knew I could barely read German, let alone write it. He looked it over and said Mutter did not know if I had reached the United States, but Benjamin had returned home and told the story of our voyage up the Rhine River. If the New York police had found me, she wanted to know my fate.

Superintendent Walling told me that it was important for me to write to my Mutter. He said, "I don't know why you ran away and I don't need to know, but I do know that no matter how bad things are at home, mothers love their children and want to know that they are safe. Please give it some thought and if you do write to her, I'll be sure it is delivered." William agreed that it would be the right thing to do. My stomach churned. I was determined that they would not force me to go back. I didn't know how, but I would escape and hide if they tried. William thanked Superintendent Walling and said he would help me write a letter and would bring it to him within a few days. They walked to the door and continued their conversation in whispers. I knew they were talking about me, but I had no way of knowing what they were thinking. Finally, Superintendent Walling waved good-bye to me and walked out the door.

William came back to me. I really liked William and trusted him. I wanted to please him, but I didn't know how I could write to Mutter. She surely wouldn't understand how much I needed to be free from Vater's strong control. William asked if I needed help. His tone was kind and not threatening, and I was glad to accept it. He took a clean, white sheet of paper out of his desk and dipped his pen in the inkwell.

"I don't know what to say," I confessed.

"Why don't you start with, 'Ich liebe dich, Mutter,'" he suggested. We worked on the letter for a long time. With William's help, the letter was completed and ready to send. I told my mother that I loved her, but I wanted to stay in America. I told her about the kindness of the Schultz family and that I was learning English. I signed my name, and with my permission, William wrote a few lines introducing himself and his family to Mutter and giving her their address.

We finished the letter and William sealed it. Mary and the girls returned home with fresh fruits and vegetables from the market. This wonderful family's love was more than I deserved. I loved my Mutter, but our home in Hechtsheim never had this warm feeling. William and Mary were not harsh with their children, or with me. I knew they were disappointed that I did not go to classes or have a job, and I felt guilty about that, but they seemed to understand that I needed time to adjust and learn.

The next day William took my letter to work to give to Superintendent Walling. I hoped the letter would satisfy him and that I would not have to write any more.

Days and weeks passed. I tried very hard to find a job so that I could earn money to repay William, but I had many disappointments. At last, I convinced a vendor to let me help at the market. I did not know how to count money or speak to the customers, so that limited my work to stacking and sorting. The little experience I had working with Siegfried in the orchards at home helped. I could recognize the best fruits and place them near the front of the display so that customers would see them first. I worked hard, watching and learning quickly. William and Mary helped me learn about money, too. I paid them a large part of the money I made, and I still felt like it was not enough, but at least I was able to give them something. Each week William would put the money I paid him into a small bag he kept in his desk.

Sundays were especially uncomfortable for me. William, Mary, and the girls ate breakfast and then dressed in their nicest clothes to attend church. They asked me if I'd like to come, but I always said no. After all, I was Jewish, and not a devout one at that. I was not interested in G_d[1], not even the Christian God.

One day a letter came from Hechtsheim. William handed me the envelope and I went to my room to read it. It was exciting to

---

[1] Orthodox Jews believe that God's name is too holy for humans to write so they leave out the vowel "o" in their manuscripts.

receive news from home, but the content of the letter left me with conflicting emotions. Mutter, though happy to hear that I was safe, begged me to come back home. Hadn't she read the part where I said I wanted to *stay*? She included a note of gratitude to the Schultz family. She ended the letter with the words, "We forgive you."

I closed the letter and went to find William. He was sitting on the front porch reading. I didn't want to interrupt his thoughts. Neither my Vater nor my older brothers ever just listened, but William and Mary always seemed to have time to talk with me. William looked up from his book and invited me to sit with him. He put a marker in the book and asked me what was on my mind. I showed him the letter and let him read it. After he finished, he said, "So, what do you want to do now?"

"I want to stay," I told him.

"Do you want to write again?"

"No!" I said sharply.

"Well, Michael, as long as you continue to help, and pay us when you can, you can stay here, but we know you will have to make a life for yourself sooner or later. I can't do it for you." It seemed like I was disappointing him again, but I just didn't have the desire to look back. I wanted to look forward. "Let me know how I can help," William said, and he went back to his reading.

I started to think again about Joseph and the promise of a job in Peoria, Illinois. If I earned enough money to buy a train ticket, I could head west. I didn't know how much money I would need or how long it would take to save it. I didn't know where the train station was or how to get there. I listened carefully at the market for anyone who talked about trains or going west.

In October we heard about a huge fire in Chicago, Illinois. How far was that from Peoria? Many people died and much of the city was destroyed. The rumor was that a cow knocked over a lantern in a barn and the straw caught on fire. I couldn't imagine a fire burning down a whole town. I would like to see that. We heard of a great demand for wood to rebuild. Forests as far away as Pennsylvania were being called upon to supply the wood for Chicago. Now that would be interesting, I thought, to work in a lumber camp.

My employer at the market trusted me now to deliver groceries. We would load the food in a cart and I would push it to the house where the customer lived and unload it for them. This was harder work for me, but I learned to find the right addresses. The customers sometimes gave me tips, and this, added to my small wages, gave me more to give the Schultz family and to save for a train ticket.

In November I turned fifteen years old. My adopted family celebrated with me by making a nice dinner. Mary had noticed that the clothes I brought from Germany were getting tight and wearing thin, so she made me a shirt and promised to make more. William bought

me a heavy winter coat. He said I would need it there in New York. I appreciated everything they had done.

I didn't know what they were talking about, but a holiday called Christmas was coming soon. I knew it was time for Hanukkah at home. I missed the candles and the gifts. Christmas also involved gifts, but only on one day. The Schultz family planned to go to church on the night before Christmas, and they sang special songs about "peace on earth and good will toward men." I had no idea what those words meant, but they sounded nice. They also talked about the birth of a baby a long time ago. That sounded nice too, but I did not understand at all.

The Schultz family gave each other gifts on Christmas Day, but I didn't. Mary gave me another shirt and William bought some pants for me. The girls gave me small gifts. Young Mary had knitted some gloves for me, and Jennie gave me a stick of candy. I needed them and thanked the family for their gifts.

The weather turned bitterly cold and mounds of snow piled up. We spent most of the time inside, but occasionally I would go out with the girls and make a snowman. With William away at work, it fell to Mary to keep the house warm. She constantly fed wood into the fireplace. I helped as much as I could. The snow made my delivery job miserable. I shoved and pushed the cart through the snow and carried groceries to the doors through the drifts. I determined during that time to go west before the next winter.

Chapter Five

Leaving New York

A whole year had passed since I left Hechtsheim. Except for the one letter William helped me write, I'd had no contact with my family. I rarely missed them, as I was growing accustomed to life in America. Although still barely adequate, my English skills had improved and I had learned so much. I knew that I would have to leave New York to "make a life of my own," as William had said, but I still didn't know when or how I could do that.

By making deliveries, I had become familiar with streets and landmarks around the city. I'd found the train station, and I counted my money carefully each night. In addition to the price of a ticket, I knew that I would need money for food and a room until I could find work.

One of my greatest anxieties was leaving the Schultz family. I had not discussed my plans with them, and I did not want to say goodbye. They had been so good to me, yet I was planning to slip out on a Sunday morning while they were at church. Pangs of guilt engulfed me, and I knew, if given a chance, that they would try to convince me to stay, warning me that I wasn't ready to live on my own. They were probably right, but I felt I had to leave before I became too attached to them.

As soon as the family left for church on a warm summer Sunday, I picked up all that I owned and wrapped it in a bedsheet. I went to the desk where William kept the money I had given him. I opened the small bag carefully. It contained enough money to last a lot longer than my savings. I emptied it onto the desk and counted over one hundred dollars. It would help me get to Peoria and get established. But the words my Vater read from the Torah rang in my ears. *Do not steal.* I knew I couldn't take money that rightfully belonged to my friend William. I put every coin back in the bag, closed it securely, and returned it to the desk. Before I could change my mind, I walked out the door and down the street in the direction of the train station.

***

Screeching brakes alerted me that the train was coming to a stop. Morning had dawned again. I had slept in a seat all night and had no idea where I was. As I looked out the window, I saw high hills,

waterfalls, and lots of trees. The beauty of it even reminded me of home a little.

How far had the train traveled from New York? I had tried to buy a ticket to Peoria, Illinois, but the man at the ticket window said I barely had enough money to get to Pennsylvania. I'd have to get off at a town called Altoona. I bought the ticket, realizing that I would have to find work if I wanted to get to Illinois.

Hours later the man who had taken my ticket walked down the aisle and announced, "Altoona!" in a loud voice. He looked at me and said, "This is your stop." I grabbed the bedsheet with my clothes and walked to the door and down the steps to a wooden platform. Other passengers met family members or friends and exchanged warm greetings. The awful feelings of loneliness that had almost vanished during my time at the Schultz home returned with a vengeance. What was I going to do now? I wanted to cry, but fifteen-year-old males are supposed to be men, not babies.

Hungry now, I looked around for a place to eat. I had only a few coins left in my pocket, but maybe they would be enough to buy an apple or a little bread. People packed the depot, either arriving or leaving, so I dodged through the crowd, went down the steps to the dirt road, and walked toward the closest buildings.

At the mercantile store I chose an apple and handed the clerk a nickel. I asked if I could have a job to earn money for my food and

board. The clerk did not give me the answer I had hoped for. Instead, he said that the lumber companies were hiring.

"It's hard work, but they pay good," he said, sizing me up as I ate my apple. I remembered the stories about the fire in Chicago and wondered if the trees here would be going there to rebuild the city. The clerk directed me to the end of the street to the lumber company's office.

After I answered a few questions, they put me right to work. I had no experience using the saws and tools, so I worked among other boys my age whose job it was to carry and stack logs onto wagons or train cars. Some of the logs were delivered to a mill where they were cut into planks and shipped to unknown places. At the end of the day my muscles burned, and I couldn't remember when I had ever been so tired. I was even too tired to eat supper. The company had bunkhouses where we slept. I threw my bedsheet bag on the top bunk, climbed up the ladder, and fell immediately to sleep.

I awakened early with the bright sun and the noise of feet hitting the floor. One of the boys said, "You better get up quick before breakfast is gone." I followed him out the door to a table set up outside that contained all sorts of food. Many of the boys had already eaten their fill and wanted to work before the heat of the day. They told me there would be food again at suppertime, but only after the boss blew a whistle signaling the work was over. Day after day, the routine continued. On Friday I stood in line to collect my pay and then stashed

it in a sock. I planned to move on to Illinois as soon as I had enough money, but for now I had no choice but to work.

I thought about Joseph and the job he'd promised in his grocery store in Peoria. Surely it would be easier than lifting wood all day. I wondered how far Peoria was from here. How much money would I need for a ticket? I was making twenty dollars per week, but I had to purchase more clothes and shoes. The lumber company provided food on the workdays, but I had to buy my own meals on my days off. I didn't have time to make friends, and besides, the families of Altoona did not associate with laborers at the lumber camp. I was just biding my time until I had enough money to move on, and I hoped that would happen before winter.

In early November the chilly wind cut through my jacket and I was grateful for the heavy coat the Schultz's had given me. I took my sock out from under my pillow and counted the money. I had one hundred dollars. I felt sure that someone had stolen some of my money while I was working, but how could I prove it? I should have at least twice that amount. Apparently, taking other people's money did not torment every man's conscience as it did mine. Of all the rules from home I wanted to be free of, this one—forbidding stealing—stayed firm in my mind. It seemed best to leave this place before thieves had a chance to take more, so I bought a ticket on the next train to Peoria, hoping Joseph would let me stay with him until I got settled again.

Chapter Six

Peoria

Leaving without notice became easier and easier for me. What would the lumber boss think when I didn't show up? Maybe that happened a lot and he was used to it. Since I hadn't stolen anything, he wouldn't take the time to look for me. He probably didn't care, except that now he was short one worker.

As I gazed out the train window, it occurred to me that Joseph might have totally forgotten me. It had been well over a year since our time on the *Graf Bismarck*, and I had not written to him. At the very least, he wouldn't be expecting me. I tried to remember his last name, but I couldn't. How would I find him without it? How many Josephs could there be in Peoria?

A gentleman sitting near me shook his newspaper so it wouldn't fold over. My eye caught the date on it—November 14, my birthday. I was sixteen years old. I had no one to celebrate with unless I could find Joseph. My last birthday had given me good memories, and I liked how the Schultz family had given me gifts. I was wearing the warm coat and gloves they gave me even now. That must be love, I thought. Sadness and loneliness overwhelmed me. I longed to be loved like that again. Where could I find it? I hoped Joseph's family would take me in like the Schultz's had.

The train ride seemed much longer than my previous one. We traveled all day, stopping at small towns along the way. The landscape had changed from the forests and mountains in Pennsylvania to rolling hills and farmland. As the sun set, I saw an occasional light from a house or barn. I had not thought to bring any food, and my stomach ached. The conductor noticed my discomfort and asked me if I was hungry. I nodded and he left. A few minutes later he came back with a fried chicken leg, a carrot, and a canteen with water. I gave him a quarter and thanked him. The food tasted so good. Later as I sat watching the scenery, I thought maybe he had shared his own dinner with me, and if so, how kind that was.

My eyelids drooped. I rested my head against the window and fell asleep. The next thing I knew, the train had stopped again. "Peoria, Illinois," the conductor's voice boomed out. I grabbed my bedsheet knapsack and exited the train. In the darkness it appeared that Peoria was much larger than Hechtsheim, but not nearly as large as New

York. I looked for a place to sleep for the night, planning to look for Joseph in the morning. I found a small wooded area near the train tracks that looked adequate, and I lay down under the stars. "Moennighoff," I said out loud, hoping no one heard. That was Joseph's last name. Remembering relieved my mind enough to allow me to drift off, full of hope that I'd be able to make a life for myself here.

***

Hunger, my constant companion, woke me the next day. Where could I eat with the little money I had? I crossed the tracks to a hotel across from the station, walked in, and sat down. A waitress came with her pad and pencil and asked what I would like. She pointed toward the board on the wall with English words on it, but I still couldn't read English well so I didn't know what it said. This was going to be harder than I had thought. She seemed to understand my problem and tried to tell me the choices using hand motions as she talked. I ordered eggs and pancakes. She turned in my order and returned with fresh milk. It tasted so good.

"Are you new to town?" she asked.

I nodded my head. "Do you know a place where I can work?"

She thought for a moment, then said, "Maybe you can ask Mr. Summers. He owns the general store. It's not far down the street. And even better, he speaks German." She slipped her pad into the pocket of

her white apron, smiled at me and went to the kitchen, returning a few minutes later with my food. I took my time and enjoyed every bite, not knowing when I would eat again. When she brought the bill, I carefully counted out the correct change.

"How do I get to the general store?" I asked. She walked to the door with me, pointed to a building a short distance down the street, and went back to her work.

I walked through the open door of the general store where a tall stocky man with an apron swept the wood floor with a broom. "May I help you?" he said with a strong German accent. In only a few moments I had learned that Fred and his sister, Sophie, ran the store. Their parents had come to Peoria from Hanover, Germany, and both Fred and Sophie had been born here. After their parents died, Fred and Sophie decided to keep and run the general store. Fred said he could use my help for a while, but he couldn't pay much.

I asked him if he knew Joseph, and to my surprise, he did. According to Fred, Joseph was the supplier of his flour. He lived only two blocks from Fred and Sophie's house. "I'll take you there after I close up the store if you like," Fred said. "I think Joseph will be at the mill now." I stayed the rest of the day and helped stock the shelves for Fred. The store had a steady stream of customers, and Fred and Sophie waited on each one with friendly service. After helping Fred close up the store, I walked home with him. Sophie had gone home earlier to cook. They invited me to stay and eat with them, and I gladly

accepted. Sophie had made beef stew and hot rolls, and had baked an apple pie for dessert. It tasted wonderful.

"We need to wait until Mr. Block leaves before we go to see Joseph," Fred said, a concerned look on his face.

"Who is Mr. Block?" I asked.

"Joseph's stepfather. He owns the saloon, and he can be mean sometimes. I don't know how Joseph and his sisters put up with him, not to mention Charlie."

"Who is Charlie?" I asked.

"I thought Joseph was your friend. Don't you know he has three sisters and a half brother?" Fred's face registered a hint of suspicion.

"No," I said. We met on the ship to America."

"That must be around the time Mrs. Block died. He demanded that Joseph come and get his sisters," Fred explained. "You'll understand when you see him."

After dark, Fred and I walked down the street. Fred's eyes darted around, looking for signs of Mr. Block. When we arrived I could see Joseph through the window. He carried a young lady in his arms and set her down in a chair. It was obvious that she was unable to

walk. We knocked on the door and a girl around the age of twelve answered the door.

"Who is it, Margaret?" Joseph asked.

"It's Mr. Summers and another man," she said. Joseph came quickly to the door. When he saw me, his jaw dropped, then he smiled and said, "Michael! I can't believe you actually came. Welcome to Peoria."

Fred made a move to leave, and I assumed he wanted to give Joseph and me time to reconnect, but to my surprise, Joseph said, "Please stay." Fred seemed to understand, and he sat down.

A young girl and boy dashed into the room, interrupting us. "Joseph, who is this?" the boy asked. Joseph told them I was his friend, then told them to get ready for bed. They scurried away.

"You'll have to excuse me, Michael, I need to tuck them in. Let me introduce you to my sisters, Louise and Margaret." I nodded at the girls, who peeked under their eyelashes at me and smiled. "Girls, would you entertain our company while I put Frieda and Charlie to bed?" Joseph left, and Margaret offered some fresh cookies to Fred and me from a plate on the table. The girls were polite, and very pretty. Louise asked where I had met her brother, and I told her we were on the ship together. I hoped she wouldn't ask about my family, but before she had a chance, Joseph returned.

"We both had our secrets didn't we?" he said to me. Turning to Fred, Joseph asked, "Could my friend stay with you and Sophie while he's here? I'm sure he would appreciate your hospitality. You understand, right?" He gave his neighbor a knowing look.

"Of course," Fred said.

"I'll explain it all to Michael and we will come back to your house before Charles comes home."

"That will be fine. I'll see you later, Michael. Do you want to work at the store tomorrow?"

"Sure," I said. Thank you."

Fred left and went back to his house. Louise and Margaret excused themselves, both claiming to be tired from a long day. Joseph helped Louise to their room. "Good night," they both said as Margaret closed the door. Joseph grabbed another cookie for himself and one for me as he returned. He pointed toward the door and suggested we go outside. I followed his lead.

"Yes, I know," he said. "I didn't mention all of this, did I?"

"Fred said your mother died and your stepfather made you come back to help."

"That's about it. I couldn't leave my sisters with this mon— oh, never mind. As you can see, my sister Louise needs me, and

Margaret and Frieda are so young. Charlie is a sweet boy and his father doesn't have any time for him. Such a shame! My stepfather, Charles, runs the saloon. Do you know what kind of people he is around every night?"

"No," I said honestly.

"Well, good thing you don't. They are all sorts of bad. I have to be here for these kids." I began to see that my visit had come at a very difficult time, and that Joseph was under a lot of pressure. "I really didn't lie about the candy making. In Germany, I was learning to make candy and I thought I could continue here. Dear Mrs. Schmidt who lives next door makes candy, and the kids love her. She helps with Louise when I have to work. The job at the flourmill is more practical than making candy. I take the kids to Mrs. Schmidt's house when I leave for work. Charles is asleep by then. I get home as soon as I can before Charles wakes up. The children make him angry, and it's even worse when he drinks. I have to be here to protect them as much as I can. I'm afraid Charles will hurt them, but I don't have enough money to move all of us away from here. Anyone who tries to help gets hurt, too. That's why you can't stay here. Do you understand?"

"Yes," I said. I wished I could help. This made my running away from Hechtsheim seem so selfish. My father was strict, but not like this. My friend had chosen the noble way. He loved his sisters and put their care ahead of his own needs. It was clear to me that I would need to move on. Joseph didn't need another person to support, and I was undependable and unable to support myself, much less anyone

else. Joseph and I talked for a long time. He suggested that I go to Chicago.

"I hear there is a lot of work there. Rebuilding from the fire." It really didn't matter to me where I went, because I knew I would be alone. I told Joseph I needed to think about it. Joseph suddenly seemed anxious, and told me it was time to leave. Charles would be coming back soon, most likely drunk. I needed to be gone by then.

I walked back to Fred's house and knocked softly on the door. He opened it and welcomed me. He gave me a blanket and a pillow and showed me to a cot in the corner of their living room. "Good night," he said. "I'll see you in the morning."

When I woke, I heard noise in the kitchen and found Sophie preparing a big breakfast. The aroma of fresh bread filled the room and made my mouth water. Fred had milked their cow and carried in a large glass jar of fresh milk. He retrieved another chair from his room and invited me to sit down for breakfast. "It's a long time until dinner, so you need to eat. But first, we pray." Sophie joined us, and Fred said a prayer. It reminded me of the Schultz family and their prayers before meals. I certainly didn't understand, but it felt so warm and comfortable with these people. They accepted me without question, but guilt plagued me and I was uncomfortable accepting their kindness. I couldn't explain it, but as wonderful as they were, I knew I didn't belong.

Fred and I worked all day at the store, but once again, I was already planning my departure. This time, I'd need enough money to buy a ticket to Chicago. I didn't know when or how much Fred would pay me, but in spite of the temptation, I could not steal from someone who had been so good to me. I watched the trains come and go every day and paid attention to the conductors' booming announcements of the destination cities. The trains fascinated me.

As I worked in the store, I became familiar with the candies that Fred sold. They came from a company in Chicago called Bunte Bros. and Spoehr, 416 State St., Chicago, Illinois. If I made it to Chicago, I would try to find that company.

***

I'd been on the train all day. Finally the conductor boomed, "Chicago!" I was in another new place knowing no one and having nowhere to stay, but I grabbed my knapsack confidently and walked down the steps to the platform. The fear I'd felt when I'd first stepped foot in America had disappeared, and I knew I would be able to handle whatever awaited me.

In spite of my newfound confidence, I found it harder this time to leave Fred and Sophie and Joseph. They'd been good and generous friends. Once again, I didn't say good-bye. I hoped that others would understand why I sneaked away. Perhaps I should have stayed, but I still wanted to do things my own way. I wanted to see Chicago and find the Bunte Bros. and Spoehr Candy Company.

Now that I was in Chicago, where would I go? This city reminded me of the size of New York City. I started walking and hoped I would find my way. The cold wind made me wish for a scarf and hat. This was not going to be easy.

Michael Capp

Chapter Seven

Steal Not This Handbag

For the first few weeks, I wandered the streets of Chicago. I slept outside on benches or under a bridge for shelter, along with many others. Many people still had nowhere to call home after the Great Fire. I remembered how Superintendent Walling had warned me about the gangs on the docks in New York, so I stayed away from the docks along the Chicago River. Even so, the rail yards seemed to attract undesirable people. I encountered some of the worst, most vile people, but I also met many good people whose only crime was that they had lost all hope. Women and children lived in filthy conditions and many were sick. Men fought and stole from each other. It was so depressing for me. I wasn't sure what I needed or wanted, but I knew this was not it.

I finally found the Bunte Brothers and Spoehr Candy Company and went into the office. The lady behind the desk was neat, clean, and looked kind. She smiled and asked, "May I help you?" I asked about jobs. She told me that they had all the workers they needed in the factory, but if I had a cart the company might hire me as a candy jobber.

There were two problems with this. I didn't have a cart, and even if I knew where to get one, I didn't have money to buy it. I left, more depressed than ever. I didn't know what to do.

I walked for a long time with my head down. Then I spotted something lying on the street. It appeared to be a lady's handbag. Why was it laying here? Did someone drop it? I looked around. There were many ladies, but I didn't see any without a bag and none seemed to be looking for one. I picked it up and wiped it off with my sleeve. The dirt and mud from the street covered the fine cloth. I looked around again. I hoped no one had noticed me. I stuffed the bag under my arm and went to a quiet spot behind one of the buildings to inspect my find. What would I see inside? I had never touched a lady's purse before, and my hands shook as my fingers untied the cords that held it shut. I pulled out a nice handkerchief with beautiful flowers embroidered on it. I admired the stitching for a moment, then unfolded it and laid it out on the ground. I turned the bag upside down and let the rest of its contents fall out. There was a round metal tin, a hair comb, some paper bills, several coins, and a small white card with some writing on it. I counted the money. Seventeen dollars and forty cents. I had used all

but a few pennies of the money I had earned from Fred in Peoria. This money would buy food for my hungry stomach and might even buy a small cart for me to use to begin my candy business. I was excited. I put everything back into the bag except the card. I tried to read it. It was a strange message, and I wasn't sure about some of the words. It said:

"Steal not this handbag for fear of shame,

That Amanda Fairchild is not your name.

For when you do, the Lord will say,

'Where is that handbag you stole that day?'

And when you say, 'I do not know,'

The Lord will say, 'Please step below.'

I decided that Amanda Fairchild must be the owner, but how would I find her? Would Amanda Fairchild know or even care if I kept it? Maybe she was rich and didn't need or miss her purse, but then again, maybe she was one of the ladies in the night who dressed in fancy clothes to attract men. They always seemed to have money for nice things.

It didn't really matter who the owner was. I couldn't ignore the fact that the message mentioned the Lord. I knew whoever He was, He would know and care. Maybe this Lord was the man who sold her to

other men. Even so, the warning about not stealing gave me a heavy feeling of guilt that was all too familiar. I knew I couldn't keep the money, even though I needed it so badly. No more questions. I had to find a way to return it. What a tough decision it was, though.

I had seen a police station a few blocks away, so I walked there with the pocketbook in my hands. I opened the heavy door and an officer asked if he could help me. I set the handbag on the counter and explained as clearly as I could how and where I had found it. "I do not know Fraulein Fairchild," I told him. He told me that they would keep it for three weeks and put an announcement in the newspaper. At the end of that time, if the owner had not claimed it, I could have the money. Though glad it was no longer in my possession, inside I was hoping it wouldn't be claimed.

I still had no money and no job. To add to my hunger and tiredness, I felt old. Scraping around for something to eat and somewhere to stay warm was hard work. I knew something would have to change before winter came again.

Three weeks later I decided to check with the police and find out whether the owner had claimed the handbag. It had not been claimed, and as the officer counted out the money into my hand, it seemed like a miracle. Finally I could buy some fresh food and look for a cart.

I went back to Bunte Brothers and Spoehr, talked with the receptionist again, and learned that another jobber had a small used

cart for sale for ten dollars. Within a couple of days I was in business. Early each morning I pushed my cart to the warehouse and stocked it with an assortment of candies. I learned to collect the correct amount of money from customers and found the best locations for peddling. I enjoyed working and earning my own way. At the end of each day I returned to the warehouse and settled my account. I would buy something to eat and then find a comfortable place to sleep for the night, with the cart always by my side.

The weather grew colder each day. I saw people come and go at a hotel near the intersection of Sherman and Fifth streets. One of my regular customers told me he was an agent for the hotel. His name was George Fox. George was older than me, and though he was married, his wife lived in Missouri with her family. I didn't ask why. George became my first true friend in Chicago. In the evenings George taught me how to play cards and showed me the best and most inexpensive places to eat. Other candy jobbers peddled for a company named Rueckheim. George and I occasionally enjoyed a taste of the competitor's wares. We especially liked their Fine Chocolates. It had not occurred to me that I could sell confections from more than one company, but George said, "Why not?" I soon expanded my candy selections with Rueckheim candies. Business was good. George let me stay in his room at the hotel, and as the winter weather intensified, I was glad to have a safe, warm place to stay after pushing my cart through snow-covered streets all day.

In the spring George received a letter from his wife, quit his job, and went back to Missouri. I found another room at a house on State Street, but I missed George's companionship. Loneliness replaced hunger as my greatest need.

Michael's Candy Wagon-Chicago, Illinois

Chapter Eight

Fredericka

The long winter had consumed all my strength. Until this point in my life, I had never felt so helpless and afraid. I had no one now—no one who cared about me. My parents didn't care anymore, and my brothers and sister were far away and probably hadn't thought about me for years. I was utterly alone. Then I met Freddie.

The crisp February air gave me a glimmer of hope. I took hold of my pushcart and picked up my supply of candies for the day from the Rueckheim candy factory, then walked up and down the streets looking for anyone who would buy my wares. The streets were either dusty, muddy, or snow packed, but the wooden-plank walkways raised pedestrians a foot or so above the street level.

I had to work. It was the only way I could block out the pain and keep myself busy. As I passed people, I searched their faces for any that seemed to need a touch of sweetness. I especially liked to see the delight in children's eyes at their first taste of taffy or chocolate or peppermint or any one of numerous other flavors. All I knew how to do was to peddle, so I sold more candy. The sweet tooth of the people in Chicago would sustain me.

The Rueckheim brothers made the finest confections in Chicago. Since Louis Rueckheim had joined his brother, I spent a lot of time with him creating new and delicious candies. As a jobber, my salesmanship skills helped to make their enterprise profitable. It was a perfect blend of creativity and wit.

One of my favorite locations was a corner near Lizzie Berthold's dress shop at Twenty-First and State Street. The girls who worked there often bought my candy, and their gentlemen friends were also good customers. Pretty girls, romance, flowers, candy—it all fit together. Except it wasn't my world. I didn't fit into their nice society. I was a lonely peddler with no family, no nice home, and no hope.

I pushed my cart down Van Buren Street toward the busiest part of town. I looked up at the street sign and couldn't believe I'd already arrived at State Street. I took a right turn and headed south. People filled the streets and the cold wind made them hurry a little more than usual. Just outside Lizzie's shop, a lady with a young boy called out to me. She obviously wanted a distraction that would keep her child occupied during the long, tedious job of fitting a new dress.

This lady was less concerned about her finances than her convenience. As I finished the transaction and the boy began to devour his prize—salt-water taffy—I decided to set up my wagon here for the day.

As I came to the intersection of Twenty-First and State again, a young, pretty girl was going inside. I waited, and when she came out I said, "Candy? I have the best in Chicago." The girl turned and smiled. I wondered how old she could be. She was small and petite, but her posture and poise gave her the appearance of an elegant young woman, rather than a schoolgirl.

"Why yes, I believe I would like a candy. What do you recommend?" she asked. I couldn't believe she was actually talking to me. I took my time and showed her the entire line of candy in my wagon. She listened intently, savoring each flavor in her mind and inhaling each delightful aroma. After she made her selection and completed her purchase she walked away, turned slightly, and glanced back at me. I thought I was in heaven. Her smile was contagious.

I wanted to know more about this new customer. When I thought about my broken English, rough manners, and undesirable past, I was pretty sure there was no chance she would be interested in me. She probably had plenty of young men from the wealthy families of Chicago vying for her attention. It didn't matter to me. I came to the same spot every day hoping to see her. Her? I didn't even know her name. I resolved to find out in our next encounter.

Several days passed before I caught another glimpse of my favorite candy consumer. This time, she left Lizzie's shop with another girl. The other girl must have been Lizzie Berthold herself, since she locked the door as they left. The girls chatted excitedly as they walked out the door. I overheard Lizzie say, "Oh, Freddie, the dance is going to be so much fun. You'll look great in your new dress. I can hardly wait, can you?" They walked quickly down the street and seemed not to notice my candy wagon at all, even though parked just a few feet away.

So, her name is Freddie, I said to myself. What kind of name is that for a beautiful girl? Maybe I misunderstood. Could it have been Carrie or Hattie or Sadie? Freddie sounds like a man's name. Like Frederick, my cousin or Joseph's friend, Fred. I thought about how wonderful it would be to go to a dance with her, but there was no way a candy peddler would ever be welcome at such a social event. It was fun to dream, anyway.

The next day I again found myself near Lizzie's shop, hoping to catch more information about the upcoming dance. I thought I might even see Freddie's dress. I stood outside the window and stole a quick look inside. Freddie was not there, but I saw Lizzie, pinning with precision the needed alterations on a red-and-white dress carefully positioned on a dress form. At just that moment Lizzie looked up and saw me peeking through the window. She took the pins out of her mouth and went to the door as I scurried back to my wagon. She called out to me, and I felt the pain of embarrassment. I tried to ignore her,

but she came right over to my wagon, pulled some change out of her apron pocket, and bought a peppermint stick.

"Are you interested in my work or just my customers?" she asked. I felt my face turning red and didn't answer. "I have a friend who also turns red when I ask her why she is suddenly eating more sweets."

"Oh," I replied, pretending to be uninterested, but hoping Lizzie would continue.

"Fredericka suggested that I should try your peppermint sticks next time I saw your wagon here. She was right. They are very good." With that Lizzie walked back to the shop and to her work.

I finally saw Freddie again. I was on the opposite side of the street where a large crowd had gathered to discover my newest treats. Apparently the date for the dance was imminent, because Freddie left Lizzie's shop with a large box in her arms. When the crowd thinned out, she crossed the street and came toward my cart.

"I'd like a peppermint stick," she said. I gave her the candy and she took the coins out of her pocketbook and paid me. "You know, my father would be very angry if he knew I was going to a dance. He is a very strict Evangelical Lutheran and forbids dancing."

"Where is your Papa?" I asked.

"He, Mama, and my brothers live in Dakota Territory. I came here to live with my Aunt Mari. Mama says it's much better for girls to live in the city because life is very harsh on the prairie. I am learning to be a dressmaker with Lizzie."

I ventured a little further. "Where did you live before?"

"We lived in Canada, near Niagara Falls. It was so beautiful and peaceful there. Papa was a tailor and inventor. He is so smart. He was the first to have a coal oil lantern in Chippewa Falls. Everyone in town thought he was foolish, and joked that he would probably burn our house down. But he didn't." I shivered inside. "Now he and my brothers are farming on the land he and Mama homesteaded."

I wanted to hear more. In fact, I could listen to her talk about her family forever. Suddenly, Freddie seemed to realize where she was. "I'm sorry for going on and on. I need to get back home now. Aunt Mari will be worried." She wrapped her scarf tighter around her face and walked quickly into the north wind.

I waited until Lizzie closed her shop for the evening. My heart skipped a beat as I approached. As she locked the door, I tapped her on the shoulder. She turned around, startled. "Please," I said, "tell me where the dance is."

"What?" she asked.

"I want to go to the dance."

"You cannot go," she said. "This is a private party. Only guests with an invitation are welcome."

I didn't really care. I wanted so much to see Freddie in her dress. I guess Lizzie saw my desperation. She shook her head, then finally took a pencil and paper from her bag. She jotted down an address and said, "Seven o'clock on Saturday."

Saturday finally came. I dressed in my best clothes, knowing that my best was still not going to be good enough for such an extravagant event, but I couldn't give up now. I went to the address Lizzie had given me. The large house shined with light and music poured from it. It was so festive. Guests arrived in carriages amid much laughter and excitement. Was Freddie there yet? A horrible thought crossed my mind. What if she came with another man? I decided to go in for only a few minutes and then leave as soon as I saw her. As I entered the front door behind a group of invited guests, I saw an elegantly decorated parlor. Red hearts and streamers hung everywhere. A long table was loaded with all sorts of delicate foods, and a big punch bowl sat at the end. I looked around the room for the shortest girl. In a corner near the punch bowl huddled a bunch of people who were obviously friends. They laughed and talked comfortably with each other. In the middle was four-foot-eleven-inch Freddie, dressed in the beautiful red-and-white dress. She was so pretty and seemed to be having a great time. I suddenly felt quite out of place and wondered if anyone had noticed me. I turned toward the door hoping to make a quick escape when Freddie looked up and saw

me. She immediately broke away from her friends and soon stood beside me. She took my arm and guided me to the group she had left a moment earlier. One by one, she introduced me to each of her friends. I nodded politely with each introduction. I didn't want to speak since I didn't know what was proper to say. As the music started, Freddie looked at me expectantly and began to move to the beat. The evening passed like the blink of an eye. I thoroughly enjoyed being with Freddie, but I couldn't completely relax. Although she tried to make me feel like an invited guest, I knew the truth. When the party came to an end, she kissed me gently on the cheek and slid a book into my hand.

"Please write in my autograph book," she said, and then she slipped away with her cousins.

I walked home wondering what an autograph book was. I made myself comfortable and began reading the entries. Many of the names sounded familiar. They were people to whom Freddie had introduced me just hours ago. I could tell that they all loved Freddie. There were entries by her aunts and uncles, her cousins, and even Lizzie Berthold. Some of them wrote in Frisian, a dialect of Low German. Others had attempted to use their new language—English. What could a prodigal Jewish son write that would compare to these beautiful words and sentiments? One entry disturbed me more than the others. It wasn't even words, but a picture—an elaborate drawing of a girl, possibly Freddie. Underneath the picture in the middle of the page, the words

"My Love" were written, and the initials "H.E.B." Who could H.E.B. be? Could he be a former—or possibly even a current—beau?

Well, I thought, I have to write something. So I recalled as many of the poems or rhymes I had ever heard, eliminating the obviously inappropriate ones. This is what I wrote:

Chicago Feb. 28.82
Dear Fredie

May angeles protect you
Both erly and late
And heaven assist you
In choosing a mate.

Yours truly,
Michael Capp

I read my entry over again. *What am I thinking? A peddler doesn't talk like that to a nice girl like Freddie. I barely know her and she doesn't know me at all. When she reads it, will she be angry? Will she hate me? Will she think this is a proposal?* I really regretted that I had not studied harder and learned to spell and use words correctly. I turned the page and decided to write something funny and lighter. I wrote the words from a song I heard the crew sing on the *Bismarck*. This is how it went:

Remember mi before you tub

Remember mi before you rub

And if the watter is to hot

Remember mi and forget me not

Forget mi not

Forget mi never

Till the sun

Shall set forever

Yours truly,

M. Capp

Feb 28.82

That's better, I thought. I'd planned to tear out the first page, but since someone had written on the other side of it, I left it. I didn't want her to notice a missing page. I wished I could erase it.

Several days passed before I came near Lizzie's shop again. I was not sure if Freddie would be there regularly, now that the dance dress was finished. I needed to get her book to her, though. One day as I peddled my candy near the dress shop, Freddie walked down the sidewalk from the north and went directly to my cart. It looked as if she'd come just to talk to me. I pulled the autograph book from the cart and handed it to her. I was relieved that she held the book and waited to read what I had written. What I didn't know then was how much willpower it took for her to fight the temptation to look

immediately for the freshest ink on her treasured pages. Instead, we talked for hours about the dance and everything else that came to our minds.

Chapter Nine

Newlyweds

It wasn't long before both Freddie and I knew the proposal in the book was sincere. She accepted! I wanted to get married right away before she had a chance to change her mind, but Freddie insisted that we get married in a church, and that meant plans had to be made. Lizzie and Freddie began sewing a new dress—a wedding dress.

Freddie had many friends and relatives in Chicago, but her mother and father were still in Dakota Territory. Her father and brothers spent long hours in the fields farming and developing seeds. Her mother worked hard to keep up the house on the prairie. They had to endure hot and dry summers and harsh winters. Indian attacks were still a real possibility. Daily life in the Wild West was always an adventure, and yet always risky. It was a thrill for Freddie whenever she received a letter from her parents, but she missed them and

worried about their safety. I still did not know what they thought about her choice in husbands.

On September 26, 1882, we were married at the Zion German Evangelical Lutheran church by a man named L. C. Koehler. I did not know him. Lizzie Berthold was Freddie's witness, and George Fox, who had come back to Chicago, was my witness. Freddie's aunts, uncles, and cousins attended, but neither of Freddie's parents came. It was harvest season and her father and brothers were too busy to leave. Of course no one from my family was there.

I had no idea what Evangelical Lutheran meant, but I was glad that the people there spoke German. Being Jewish, I didn't understand any of the things that were being said, but it didn't matter. I was in love with Freddie and we were married. I didn't bother to tell her about my past or that my real name was Kapp, not Capp.

I had new energy as I continued to peddle my candy. The Rueckheim brothers moved their business from place to place, gradually acquiring the latest and best confectionary equipment. When his brother was gone, Louis and I started working enthusiastically on a new candy, a molasses mixture poured over popcorn and peanuts. We stored it in wooden barrels and gave samples to our customers. People loved it.

I found out quickly that Freddie had many religious friends. They went to church at least once every week and sometimes more. I avoided as many of those meetings as I could, but I wanted to be with

Freddie and was lonely when I was at home without her. Haunting memories of my past often crept back into my mind, though, so I went to the meetings with Freddie to keep from thinking about them. One of her friends, Clara Bletsch, was the daughter of the pastor at Portland Avenue Methodist Church. Freddie enjoyed the Bletsch family and often spent time with them. I tagged along, but I didn't feel comfortable with Christians. Their beliefs were strange. Although I had given up on the G_d of my father, the Christian God was totally foreign to me.

Because Freddie and her friends had experienced the terrible Chicago fire in their youth, they had a deep compassion for people who had lost friends and family, as well as their earthly possessions, in that fire. They were always ready to help others in any way they could. Freddie cooked meals and delivered them to invalids, sewed clothes or blankets for the people who lived on the streets, and taught children Bible stories. She used the Bible and songbook her father had given her. I didn't know what gave her such a love for people, but I loved her even more for it. Her smile, as well as her happiness, was contagious. I wanted to be more like Freddie, but I couldn't make myself happy, and I knew who I really was—a miserable liar, corrupt to the core. Freddie didn't ask a lot of questions about my past and didn't insist that I go with her to her church meetings. She must have wondered what I was hiding, though, and I was sure her friends thought I was strange.

Many changes were happening in Chicago, and I heard her friends talk about a great revival in tent meetings held by a man named Dwight Moody. They were also excited about a big meeting that would take place at Niagara-on-the-Lake, Ontario, Canada, not far from Freddie's childhood home. All of this meant nothing to me.

In the beginning, Freddie and I lived in my room on Dearborn, but by the spring of 1883 we knew that we would need a larger place because Freddie told me that a baby was on the way. We moved to 3122 Emerald. The house was in a nice area and had a fenced yard. We started planning and preparing for the new arrival.

As the months passed, I sold candy all day while Freddie kept house and continued to work with Lizzie. She never complained, and she made our home comfortable. But something horrible still churned inside of me. I could not forget the things I had done in the past—the lack of respect for my parents and teachers, and the angry words and bad attitude. I hurt people and didn't even care. When people showed me kindness and love, I ran away. I wondered if I could be a good husband and father to Freddie and our baby. Would I abandon them just when they need me most? Would they fall victim to a horrible tragedy like the fire? The questions were more than I could handle. Then Freddie's voice, thoughts of the baby, or the new project with Louis Rueckheim would pull me back to the sweet things in my life.

A letter arrived from Dakota one day that did not have good news. Freddie's mother, Catherine Bludorn, had become sick, and in the early winter storms of 1883 she had died. Her father and brothers

decided that as soon as the weather improved, they would sell their land and move to Chicago. The weather had even prevented them from having a proper burial for Freddie's mother.

I worried that Freddie's grief over the loss of her mother during the last weeks of her pregnancy would make the birth difficult, but she was strong, and when her time came to deliver, everything went well. On December 28, 1883, our son Frank Heinrich Capp was born. Freddie's aunts and cousins were ever present to dote on her and the new baby.

That winter seemed to drag on forever. A new baby ought to bring joy, and yet the cold weather and mourning gave both Freddie and me a dark, dismal attitude. I had not shared with her the thoughts that continually plagued me, yet she knew something was very wrong. Day after day I was sinking, and nothing could pull me out of the deep, dark hole I seemed to be in. I quit eating and became very weak. I found it harder and harder to get myself out on the streets to sell the candy. Nothing mattered any more. My life was worthless.

Chapter Ten

The Darkness

Freddie's family treated me very well. They included me in every dinner or celebration, but I did not know how to respond to their love and I did not return their warmth.

After the death of Freddie's mother, her father, Christian Bludorn, and her younger brother, Louis, closed up their affairs in Dakota and came to Chicago. They sold their land to her older brother, Charles. They moved in with other relatives. Charles was a seed salesman, and except for the fact that his business required travel, he stayed in Freeman, Dakota Territory. We didn't see him often, but when we did he seemed friendly. Even in his grief, Freddie's father, Christian, seemed strong and kind. Christian and Louis visited our house often and loved to be with baby Frank. They were devout

Christians and went to church often. I doubt Christian would have chosen me to marry his only daughter, but he never told me that.

We moved our little family to a house on Fox Place. It had a nice yard with a fence so that we could play outside with our son when the weather permitted. My dark attitude made it difficult for me to enjoy my son, though.

I was twenty-six years old, and until that time I had never mentioned the name of Jesus. I didn't even use it in vain, as many people do. I didn't want to acknowledge Him in even a profane way. I can truly say I hated the name of the Son of God with all my heart. And yet Freddie and her friends and family always talked about this Jesus. It was all so confusing to me.

I went to meetings just to be with Freddie and to impress her family. The meetings were often held in tents and lasted for hours. One day something that was said perked my interest. The speaker presented the scripture recorded in Ezekiel 18:4: "Behold, all souls are mine: as the soul of the father, so the soul of the son is mine; the soul that sinneth, it shall die." I was really upset and even angry when I heard that man quoting the Jewish scripture. This was *my* religion's book! When I went home I searched the Jewish scriptures, which I had not touched in years, just to prove he had it wrong. I was shocked to see that what he said was exactly the same in the prophet's writing. I suddenly realized for myself that if there was a God, I was in deep trouble.

I never understood my father's G_d and had even doubted God's existence for the past ten years. I thought only about myself, and I believed I could handle life on my own. It obviously wasn't working, but I didn't want to believe it had anything to do with God. If He existed, where was this God? And how could he care about me?

I fell to the floor and said, "Oh God, if there is a God, I want to know the truth concerning these things." At once I felt my awful condition. I *knew* I was a sinner and that God's judgment was pronounced upon me. "The soul that sinneth, it shall die." It seemed like I could see this scripture *everywhere*.

I began to search the Jewish Scriptures, starting in the book of Genesis. I couldn't read Hebrew very well, because I hadn't read it for many years. I had trouble getting ahold of the thoughts, but I searched day and night. The more I read and understood the scriptures, the more the darkness would increase. I searched until I came to the sixteenth chapter of Leviticus. There I saw Yom Kippur—the Day of Atonement. I realized that was the day and the place a Jew could be saved. For on the Day of Atonement we read that a sacrifice was brought to the high priest. He placed his hand on the head of the sacrifice, confessing his sins and the sins of the people. The sacrifice being identified—or rather substituted for—both the high priest and the people, had its blood shed, and its blood was then carried within the veil into the holiest of all and sprinkled upon the mercy seat. The people on the outside were lying on their faces, waiting for the high priest to return. By the priest's return they knew that the sacrifice had

been accepted and they could go on rejoicing. The substitute was slain in the guilty sinner's stead. The guilty sinner could rejoice, knowing that his substitute was accepted before God. I then rejoiced greatly. This is the way a Jew can be saved, I thought, but my joy didn't last long, because when I looked around for an altar there was none. No altar, no high priest, no temple, no holiest of all in Chicago. My people were scattered, and darkness descended even deeper upon my soul.

I wasted away to almost a shadow. Freddie and our friends thought I was going into consumption. But no one under the sun knew what really ailed me. It was this awful thing, "The soul that sinneth it shall die." I knew *I* was the sinner. Also I knew that the righteous judgment of God hung over me, and in that condition my heart and soul could find no peace. This continued for months.

To add to my grief, Freddie became pregnant again, and on July 8, 1885, a daughter, Carrie Charlotte, was born. She was supposed to be born in August, and so she was too small. She struggled and fought to keep living, but by the end of the day she was gone. Freddie was weak with pain and sorrow and I was no help for her. My worst nightmare seemed to be coming true. Friends and family came to help and I sank deeper. They buried Carrie in a grave at Oakwood cemetery, but I could not go. The pain was too deep.

I continued to go and listen to the man who first spoke from Isaiah. I wanted to believe there was a God and that He did care. The distance from the place we lived to the place where I went to hear the word of God was about a mile. Every foot of that ground had been

sprinkled with my tears. I can also say that not one night during that whole year did I have a good night's rest. I knew the wrath of God abided upon me.

I kept searching the scriptures until I came to Isaiah 53. It starts in Isaiah 52:13, just as it does in Hebrew. It begins, "My servant shall deal prudently." I remember that my father taught me as a child that in the book of Isaiah three servants are mentioned: my servant Israel, my servant Jacob, and MY SERVANT. He said that MY SERVANT in the book of Isaiah was a reference to the Messiah. "Messiah" is the Hebrew word that is translated "Christ" in Greek. I wondered who MY SERVANT was. When I came to Isaiah 53:4 where it is recorded, "Surely, He hath borne our grief and carried our sorrows," I realized I did want to know who that was, because I had *so* much grief and *so* much sorrow.

I had not been fit to do a day's work for some time. I do not know how Freddie and Frank could stand to be with me. My heart was almost broken with grief. I lived in terror day and night, and desperately wanted to have peace. I wanted to be rid of all the sorrow that weighed upon me. I meditated long upon Isaiah 53:4, and then read the rest of the passage. "We esteemed him stricken, smitten of God and afflicted." I marveled that the Messiah should be stricken and afflicted, and that we should dare to esteem Him lightly.

The same day that I read this, an event occurred. This I must tell you in order that you may get the connecting link. About three o'clock in the afternoon I went outside. I watched as a little piece of

paper flew into the yard. I picked it up and saw an advertisement for a special sale on Bibles at Revell's Book Store. They cost three dollars and twenty-five cents each. I had never owned either an English or a German Bible, and I thought one would cost at least fifty or a hundred dollars. I ran inside to Freddie. Our finances were very limited at that time because I could not work due to my poor health and troubled soul. For almost a year I had only worked a little bit. We had only five dollars and twenty-five cents in the house and would not have any more for another week. I said to Freddie, "I can buy a Bible for three dollars and twenty-five cents. I'm going to walk downtown and get one before they are all sold out." I had no idea that a person could buy a Bible for fifteen or twenty cents. I bought a big family Bible. I esteemed it the greatest treasure I ever owned.

That evening I went into my room and read Isaiah 53 again, but now in the German language. When I got to Isaiah 53:5 I read, "He was wounded for our transgressions." I said aloud, "Oh, God, who is it that was wounded for my transgressions?" I could not understand how it could be that somebody would be wounded for my transgressions. Then I read the next clause, "He was bruised for our iniquities, the chastisement of our peace was upon Him and with His stripes we are healed." I saw substitution, but *who was it that was wounded for my transgressions*? I could not understand. I thought I would go out of my mind that night. I could bear it no longer. Up to that time, I had never mentioned the name of Jesus in my life—not even to curse with. I wouldn't dare mutter that name even as a curse. I saw I was terrified of it.

My attention focused on the next verse. "All we like sheep have gone astray." I said, "Oh, God that is me. I surely have gone astray!" I knew that for my whole life I hadn't cared at all about what God said. It wasn't important because I didn't really believe He existed anyway. Then the thought of the fifth verse came back to me again, "wounded and bruised for *me*"—this was substitution. Then I read the next clause, "We have turned every one to his own way." *Oh, how I did see my awful condition. I know I have turned my own way. I know I* never *went God's way.* And then, in awful agony of heart, I read the last clause of that verse, "God hath laid on him the iniquities of us all." My eyes were opened about the sacrifice in Leviticus 16. I saw on the Day of Atonement how Aaron laid his hand on the sacrifice, how he confessed the sins of the people, how the blood was shed, how it was accepted before God, and how man was justified; but here I saw where God laid our sins on Him! God Himself laid on somebody the iniquities of us all. I was quite out of my mind by then. *Who* can that person be? I saw that the sacrifices had ceased for over eighteen hundred years. I saw also that God's sacrifice had taken the place of the sacrifices at the temple.

I opened the New Testament. It was the first time in my life that I had read it. I opened it at John 3:16 and read, "For God so loved the world." I had never known that God loved me, for no man had told me. It was a new revelation to me. *Is it possible that God can love such an awful man as me? Such a fearful sinner?* I meditated upon it a great deal. Then I read on. "God so loved the world that He gave His only begotten Son." The thought of what was written in Isaiah 53:5

and 53:6 was very strong on my mind: "wounded for our transgressions, bruised for our iniquities, God laid on Him the iniquities of us all—God so loved the world—God gave." I could not understand what it all meant, and I think I must have spent at least an hour at that part of the scripture. At last, my eyes fell on the opposite page and I read this passage in John 1:12, "To as many as received Him, to them gave He power to become the Sons of God, even to them that believe on His name." Then I went down on my knees to pray for the first time in my life, because Jews do no pray on their knees. I said, "Lord, God, if Jesus is your Son—if Jesus is the sacrifice of Isaiah 53—if you have laid on Him my sins, my iniquities—and if you have loved me and given Jesus for me and by my accepting Jesus I can become Your child, I will accept Jesus." And immediately the awful burden of sin was absolutely *gone*!

I saw Jesus, God's sacrifice, who died in my place, right there in my room. At that moment I knew that I was accepted by God as His own dear child, as it says in the scriptures. In I John 3:2 I read, "Beloved now we are the Sons of God." I do not have to wait until death. Also in I John 5:9-13 I read His testimony of how to make God a liar: "He that believeth not God hath made Him a liar; because he believeth not the record that God gave of His Son. And this is the record that God hath given to us eternal life and this life is in His Son." And, "He that hath the Son, hath life." *I have the Son, therefore I have eternal life*. In verse 13 it says, "These things are written unto you that believe on the name of the Son of God that ye may *know* that ye have eternal life." You see, there is knowledge that this was written for that

very purpose—that I (and you) might no longer walk in darkness. My conclusion, then, was this—as I once hated the name of Jesus with all my heart, I could truly say I loved Him now.

The darkness in my soul evaporated. From that time on, I couldn't get enough of the truth in the Bible. I wanted to read every word of it. I was full of life and joy. I could work again, and my wife finally had a whole and healed man.

Michael and Freddie (Frederica) Capp

Chapter Eleven

New Beginnings

It was wonderful! I could sleep peacefully, I could eat, and I could enjoy my wife and son. As the scripture said, I was a new creation in Christ. The old had passed away, and all things were new. I also thoroughly enjoyed my work again.

When I returned to the Rueckheim's candy company, I found that they had changed, too. I would no longer use my pushcart to sell the confections, but would use a big wagon and a horse to pull it. We agreed that, over time, I would purchase the horse and wagon from the Rueckheims. My wagon contained room for a lot more candy, and I could cover a lot more area with my horse. Business was good, and since Freddie and I were again expecting a baby, the extra money would be a blessing.

Freddie was nervous to be pregnant again so soon after Carrie's death. She knew that things were different now, though. I was able to comfort her and be a good husband during this pregnancy. Although I worked until dusk, I was able to come home, feed and water the horse, and then help with Frank. He was nearly three years old now and required more attention. As soon as I tucked him into bed, I went to my room and read more of the wonderful book that led me to my Savior.

Each night new truths would fill my soul. I often shared what I was reading with Freddie, and she was thrilled to hear my joyful heart spilling over with love like never before. I couldn't wait until the next opportunity to hear the gospel preached. We went with Freddie's friends and family, and soon they became my friends, too. They saw the changes in me and knew that my faith was real. When I couldn't understand something that was said or something I had read, they patiently helped me.

I had learned from my childhood that dusk on Friday began the Shabbat, and it seemed strange to me that Christians went to church on Sunday. However, it didn't matter to me what day of the week it was if it meant I could worship the Lord that had set me free from my darkness. A man in Chicago named Dwight Moody started a new trend called Sunday school. At those meetings we were able to study the Bible together in smaller groups and learn from each other. Mr. Moody was a shoe salesman, but as his love for God and for teaching others grew, he gave up his business. Many of the principles he used in

business carried over into his teaching and preaching. In both environments, the principles worked. The church where we could go to hear Mr. Moody was called Chicago Avenue Church.

On July 3, 1886, Freddie and I welcomed another son into our growing family. We named him Edward. Edward was a delightful child from the beginning. I considered him a gift from God, and I felt God was pleased with me. This was the first time I had ever believed God actually loved and cared about me.

Louis Rueckheim was a genius. He elevated the art of candy making to a new level. The company did not carry the name Reliable and Fine Candies lightly—they truly were the best quality confections around. Louis was still working on our molasses-coated popcorn snack when, in 1887, a fire burned down the entire factory. The loss was devastating, but F. W. Rueckheim, Louis's older brother, had come to Chicago after the great fire in 1871. He had cleared debris and joined an older man in restoring his candy company. F. W. had seen businesses ruined by fire, but also believed they could do it all again. The Rueckheim's original company began with only a molasses kettle and a popcorn popper. Now nothing could be salvaged from the rubble. But the brothers worked hard, and in just a few weeks they were in business again. Within six months, they had rebuilt and moved into a building on the old property. Each step brought new machinery and processes. The next move took them to a new building on Desplaines Street where they even installed a sprinkler system.

I loved being around Louis, and I also loved watching him try new and different confections. The molasses-covered popcorn was the best, though. Louis tried different popcorns and also different ways of coating each piece of corn. When his older brother was out of town, we felt freedom to really try new things. The popcorn and peanut treat was a customer favorite, and each day several wooden barrels with the confection were loaded into my wagon.

Louis and F. W. were God-fearing men. They saw changes in me as well. Life was good and we all prospered.

At home, we found out that there would soon be yet another Capp mouth to feed. Our home was filling up quickly, but Freddie was a great homemaker. She kept our home pleasant and orderly and still had time to participate in "Bible work." Miss Emma Dreyer had established classes for mothers and children at the church, and Bible work was an extension of the lessons the women learned. The work consisted of helping the poor and needy. Freddie loved the work and found that caring for others came naturally to her. Frank and Edward often accompanied her as she visited those who needed help.

On July 16, 1888, another boy joined the family. We named him Wallace Victor Capp. Freddie found it harder to keep up with three children, and her volunteer work had to be cut back. Frank, nearly five years old, was bright and learned quickly. While her hands were full taking care of the younger boys, Freddie knew that Frank would need to attend school soon. St. Stephens, where we had been married, had a school. We decided to send Frank there, knowing that

he would be taught biblical values and manners as well as academics. So Frank, swinging his lunch pail, walked to school.

The thought kept going through my mind that I should go to school too. When I was a little boy in Germany we had a teacher for all the Jewish children in the village, but I did not want to do all the studies and was often in trouble for misbehaving, which distressed my parents to no end. Thankfully, Frank was not following in my footsteps in that respect. I had learned very little, but what I had learned was in German and Hebrew. Most of the things that were useful to me as an adult, I'd learned while living with the Schultz family in New York. Now I wanted to learn to read the Bible in English and to study everything it contained. I knew it would be hard work.

For two years Dwight Moody had been considering a school to train common men to do Christian work. His idea was to have the students study in the mornings with ministers of different denominations presenting good Bible lectures, then they were to visit every family in their area district. Every night they would learn to preach the simple gospel themselves. So in February 1887, he opened the Chicago Evangelical Society. Attending school seemed an impossible goal for me because of my poor English and also due to the fact that my family of five needed me to work. So I continued to sell candy and study the Bible in the evenings.

The desire to preach the gospel never faded, though. Could God use a man such as me? As I read the stories of Peter, Matthew,

and Paul, I saw that God used men who were not that different from me. Maybe—just maybe—He would use me someday. My heart and thoughts turned increasingly to evangelism, but the obstacles did not go away. Freddie encouraged me to be patient. She said that God would reveal His plan for me in time. Patience had never come easily to me.

On March 13, 1891, God blessed us with a daughter. The delivery was difficult for Freddie, as our "little girl" was not really little at all. Jeanette Edna Capp entered this world weighing a whopping twelve pounds. She was healthy and strong. Any fears we had from the memories of Carrie's death were gone. Jeanette was here to make her mark on the world. She had three brothers to protect her, but she took care of herself just fine.

Chicagoans were preparing for a big event. The World's Fair was coming to the "windy city." They called it the Colombian Exposition in honor of Columbus discovering the New World. Buildings were constructed, people from all over the world appeared in the city, and a huge round wheel was set up to take people on a ride high above everything. All these new sights, sounds, and smells were almost too much to take in.

Louis Rueckheim saw this as a perfect time to introduce his molasses-peanut-popcorn treat to the world. Production at the factory exploded to meet the needs of the jobbers on the streets as well as the new customers visiting the fair. They needed a name for the snack, so one day as a jobber sampled it, he said, "That's a cracker jack." And

so the name was born. I could not take credit for Cracker Jacks. That was all to Louis' credit, but I felt I'd had a part of the success since I had sold it from my wagon and promoted it in the streets of Chicago. I knew things would change when the world got a taste of this treat.

The World's Fair also created a platform from which the Chicago Evangelical Society could spread the gospel of Jesus to people from all over the world. The fair brought the cultures of China, Sudan, Tunisia and Algiers, the South Sea Islands, Germany, Lapland, Turkey and Persia, and other far away places to the streets of Chicago. Different religions and philosophies vied for the attention of the people. Add to that the shocking spiels of the sideshows. How could the message of salvation compete? But it was a great opportunity, and we believed that God would draw some to listen and find the peace their souls yearned for. This was exciting for me, so I signed up to hand out flyers and tracts about our tent meetings as I peddled my candy.

God had blessed me immensely in the six years since I had met Jesus on my bedroom floor. Financially, Freddie and I were doing fine. We had moved to a larger house on Fifth Street just before Jeanette was born. Now Edward was ready to go to school too. Even with two of the boys gone for part of the day, Freddie's hands were full. I supported her as much as I could and took the boys to school in the wagon before I started my candy route. The excitement of the fair was all the boys could talk about. The thought of going to the top of the world on a giant wheel crowded out any talk of everyday things. I

heard constantly, "Daddy can we go? Please, please, please!" I knew it would be the chance of a lifetime, but I also worried about the images that would be impressed on their little minds at the fair.

My heart still dreamed of spreading the gospel full time. I believed God had planted that desire within me, and I knew that if it were to happen there would have to be a miracle. Freddie and I discussed the possibility and prayed for God's will concerning this. We could see only one way for me to be able to afford the Bible institute. That would be to sell my candy business.

In January I cut my ties with the Rueckheims and became an independent candy jobber. Now I could sell my horse and wagon and have enough to cover the family's expenses while I went to school. A man from Racine, Wisconsin, William Stadter, had wanted to buy my business, so in March 1892 I sold it to him. I enrolled in Moody Bible Institute that same day.

I did not know where God would lead us from here, but I knew He was calling me into the ministry. Freddie knew it too, but selling our only source of income required a giant leap of faith.

Michael Capp Tent Meetings

Chapter Twelve

Moody Bible Institute

So now what? The future was unknown and yet I knew it held hope and good things for my family and me. I was excited at the prospect of learning all the rich bits of truth and wisdom God had stored for us in His word and then sharing it with others. At the Institute, the Bible was the foundational book and I read and studied it like I had never studied any book before. According to Dr. Moody's design, we sat in a lecture from eight o'clock in the morning until midday. The morning lectures stimulated my mind and whetted my appetite for more. Dr. Torrey conducted most of the lectures, but other teachers from many different denominations of churches came to teach us from the Bible.

Classes began with an introduction to the Bible. We learned that the Bible is the inspired Word of God, how it is structured, and

how to go about studying it. We studied topics such as God, the divinity of Christ, the Holy Spirit and His work, the fall of man, sin, redemption, justification, adoption, repentance, faith, good works—the list went on and on. We read and discussed every book in the Bible, which included all the Torah books, which I had read but not appreciated in my childhood.

One of my favorite parts of the day was hearing other students' analyses of what we had read. People from all walks of life attended those classes—among them businessmen, construction workers, firemen, police, farmers, accountants, doctors, and lawyers. I saw that the need for salvation was not limited to poor, rebellious people like me, but also the wealthy and socially prominent. I loved that about Jesus. The gospel spread across every boundary. Rich, poor, old, young, men, women—all races, cultures, and nationalities stood on equal ground at the foot of the cross.

We were encouraged to visit people in our neighborhoods in the afternoon, and in the evening to preach the simple gospel wherever possible—in local churches or in tent meetings. As the World's Fair brought massive crowds, we had little trouble finding an audience. Many heard us speak and some received the gift of salvation. We grew in faith and in our ability to share the gospel.

Music was a big part of our instruction, and we learned to use it in our meetings. Songs and hymns often seemed to stir the Holy Spirit within people's hearts and prepared them for the preaching of the Word. We had a songbook that we used both at the Institute and in our

meetings. We used a piano when available, but most of the time we sang "a cappella." Freddie and I taught our children the songs, and Frank especially loved to sing about Jesus.

The school had a dormitory for single men, and many of the students lived there. I, however, had a home and family to consider. Freddie supported and encouraged me, but much of the work at home fell on her shoulders again. Taking care of the boys and Jeanette drained most of her energy. Besides this, she was pregnant again, and I knew she was concerned about how we would feed one more mouth. We had a garden, and sometimes people from church or Freddie's family would bring us food. We were so grateful for their help. Freddie managed our meager finances and was able to keep our expenses to a minimum. She sewed most of the clothes for the family, and the older children passed down their outgrown shirts, pants, and shoes to the younger ones.

Probably the most frustrating thing for Freddie was when I would get so involved talking to someone that I'd invite them to our home for a meal without thinking about her. She adapted by learning to prepare enough food for an occasional guest. She welcomed strangers and made them feel comfortable during those impromptu visits. The children also came to enjoy new faces at the dinner table.

I formed special bonds with several people as we studied and grew in our faith together at Moody. One in particular was Caleb Baker. C. J., as he preferred to be called, was a partner in a tent and awning business. During the great fire in 1871, their company was in

danger of being swallowed by the flames. Since they were located close to the river, they took their machines and began to make large bags. They sealed the seams to make them waterproof and then put their machines and bolts of fabric into the bags, sewed them shut, and threw them into the river. In that way, their business was saved. Although the building was gone, they were able to pull the bags out of the river once the fire was out. They set up their machines on the street and began sewing tents and shelters for those who had nowhere to live. Throughout the ordeal, C. J. felt God's leading and protection over him and his family. Because of this he felt blessed, and set about to help others.

C. J. was an excellent student of the Bible. He was associated with the Plymouth Brethren and had a very humble spirit. His writing and examination of scripture drew me to him and we became close friends. He designed a chart that the Lord inspired. The chart contained scripture and pictures, and his diagram was easy for his audiences to follow as he preached. He called it "The Two Roads and the Two Destinies."

In spite of all the wonderful things happening in my life, one issue still haunted me about my past. Since my father was a rabbi and knew the Torah very well, how did he miss the prophecies of Messiah, and how could my people, the Jews, have missed the fulfillment of those prophecies in the life of Jesus? My heart broke when I thought of my siblings and cousins who were still unaware of the good news that Jesus is the Messiah. I wondered how I could tell them. I wrote a letter

to my home in Hechtsheim. I wondered if anyone would even care what had happened to me. Deep down inside I didn't expect to get a response, but I had to try. It had been over twenty years since I had talked with any of them, and I wasn't even sure whether any still lived in Hechtsheim.

I knew there were other Jews in Chicago who had never heard of Jesus. Could I find them and begin sharing the story of salvation with them? At Moody's Institute, we were encouraged to speak, and yet what interest would a Jew have in these meetings? Only a few years earlier I had hated the name of Jesus and was offended at the suggestion that He was MY SERVANT. Would any Jews open their hearts to that message if I spoke it?

I shared my concern with Freddie and she, as always, supported me. She talked with her friend Clara Bletsch about my concern. Soon I found myself talking with Clara's father, Jacob Bletsch, who was the pastor at a small Methodist church on Ashland Avenue. Rev. Bletsch recognized my passion and interest in sharing the gospel with my people. Grateful for his help, I knew that God had opened this door for me.

So, in April 1892, I began holding meetings at the Methodist church on Thursday evenings and Saturday afternoons. The church was very supportive of my mission to the Jews and helped get it started. Posters and flyers were printed, and of course the statement "Come hear a Jewish man who speaks about Jesus" grabbed the attention of many. People were curious about this, and fifty people

attended the first meeting. Eight of them were Jewish. I began to outline the scriptures as I had encountered them in my own salvation, and the audience listened intently.

On Saturdays the attendance grew to about sixty. Some faces were new, and a few more were Jewish. At the end of each meeting I stayed to answer questions and waited for opportunities to lead any who were willing to confess Jesus as their own Savior.

In a few months an average of sixty people attended each meeting and at least twenty-five were Jewish. In the first few weeks about a dozen of the Jews who heard made a confession of Christ as their Savior, and six of those were baptized. I knew that about one hundred people who came to our meetings were now under deep conviction. They would stay and inquire more. I knew what a big step it was for a Jewish person to confess that they believe Jesus is the Messiah. They often risked being rejected by their family. Even though I knew the cost, the Lord filled my heart with joy for the people who received the truth about Jesus and were saved—Jew and Gentile together.

By summer I added a Sunday meeting for children. My own children came, of course, and with Freddie's help these meetings were very popular. We started teaching at the Sunbeam Mission, and those children actively brought Jewish children to hear. Some of the parents came to the adult meetings and received Jesus as their Messiah.

In October 1892 Freddie gave birth to our fourth son. We named him Bert Matthew. Our lives were so full—me with my studies and meetings and Freddie with the children. We needed to move into a yet bigger house to accommodate our growing family, so just before Bert's birth, we moved to a house on Iowa Street. It was obvious that I would need to finish my studies at Moody soon and go back to a job that could sustain our family. I knew there was still a lot for me to learn, and yet my time at the Institute gave me the springboard and tools I needed to continue.

News of the meetings at the Methodist church spread, and I was asked to come and speak occasionally at other churches and meetings. I would sometimes receive a small offering that helped our family, but I knew it would not be enough.

Chapter Thirteen

The World's Fair

When I sold my candy business, I felt like that part of my life was completely in the past. And to a certain extent, it was. Although no longer the rebellious, selfish, desperate man I once was, I was far from being a responsible husband and father. We had lived on so little money during my time at Moody. I saw in the Bible that if I do not provide for my family, I am worse than an unbeliever (I Tim. 5:8). It was clear to me that I needed to work and earn enough money to feed my growing family. The only job I knew was selling candy, so I talked to Louis Rueckheim again.

The World's Fair had fully opened and large crowds of people swarmed the area. I took Freddie and the children to the fantastic Columbian Exposition. It was a sacrifice to pay twenty-five cents for each of us to get into the fair. Even with Jeanette and Bert getting in

for free, the dollar twenty-five was a lot for our family. When we found out that it was an additional fifty cents to ride on the big wheel, we just had to be content with seeing the wheel and imagining how the world would look from the top. The boys were disappointed.

All the big buildings were a gleaming white, and so the name "White City" was often used, referring to the grand display of architecture and culture. The fairground was huge, 690 acres total. There was no way we could see all of it. Freddie and I alternated carrying the baby and holding Jeanette's hand. Frank and Edward kept Wallace from wandering away or causing trouble.

We walked for hours taking in the displays and sights. Over forty-six countries were represented, each with its own "village." Germany's culture was familiar to Freddie and me, but the displays from Egypt, Mexico, Ireland, China, Italy, and many others filled our senses with sights, sounds, and smells we had never imagined. Forty-six states and territories also had displays. From the oranges grown in Florida to the Alaskan Eskimo village and Hawaiian hula dancers, there was a new surprise at each booth. Our children were wide-eyed with wonder and awe.

Freddie was thrilled to see all the household innovations at the Women's Building. "Can you believe they have a machine that will wash clothes?" she asked, overwhelmed by the idea. Since her father was the first to use coal-oil lanterns in Chippewa Falls, she was fascinated with the phosphorescent lamps as well as the new-fangled

electrical lights. It seemed that *everything* could be powered by electricity—whole kitchens, whole houses, even whole cities!

In the machinery buildings we saw the plows, combines, and reapers that I had heard about. Mr. McCormack was very active at Moody and contributed large amounts of money to the Institute, but I had no idea that he was responsible for creating these monstrous machines that would have made the Bludorn's farming work in Dakota much easier.

I was interested in all the new food products. A hot cereal called Cream of Wheat; a new gum called Juicy Fruit; Quaker Oats; a pancake mix; and of course the Rueckheim's molasses-popcorn treat—all were drawing new customers. Within just a few months, these products could become known all over the world. I thought that if people from all those countries got a taste of these products at the fair, production would have to increase significantly to keep up with the orders.

At the Rueckheim's booth the new popcorn treat was extremely successful. I thought I might be able to work at the booth for a few hours a day and still have time to preach when I was asked, as well as continuing the meetings at Ashland Avenue Methodist Church. Louis agreed to let me work at the booth during the summer and early fall of 1893. Meanwhile, he would watch for an opportunity for me to share a candy jobber job. Maybe after the fair one of the salesmen could use an assistant if business was as good as we expected.

As we were leaving the fair, another tent drew the attention of the boys. The signs said "Wild West Show." Bill Hickok and several others, including a girl, were demonstrating horse riding, roping, and shooting skills. I had to admit that it was exciting, but neither Freddie nor I wanted the boys to get too interested in playing with guns. Nettie saw the girl named Annie shooting over her shoulder using a mirror to see her target. Her shot was perfect. Nettie told her brothers, "Girls can do it, too!"

Our children were growing quickly. Frank was ten years old, Edward was seven, Wallace was five, Jeanette was three, and Bert was one. Each had their own personalities, and I knew that I would need to take a more active role in training them. Frank was smart and responsible. He was a big help to Freddie and often watched over the younger boys to keep them out of trouble. At school Frank was a good student and always did his work on time. Edward was a quiet and gentle child, loved by everyone. His tender heart made him a joy to be around. He was a good student but was often found daydreaming. Frank and Edward spent most of their days at school.

After the fair, Frank and Edward were taught to recite a declaration of loyalty called "The Pledge of Allegiance." Each morning their teachers led them in saying, "I pledge allegiance to my flag and to the Republic for which it stands, one nation, indivisible, with liberty and justice for all." It was a lot of big words and I really couldn't explain what they meant, so I left that to their teachers. It is to show our love for our country, they said. I did appreciate America and

the wonderful life I was allowed to live here, however I knew that God was really the one who deserved the credit.

At the age of five, Wallace concerned me quite a bit. Of all the children, he reminded me most of myself. He had a rebellious spirit. Our best efforts to teach him seemed to fall on deaf ears. Freddie was frustrated and tired. Often by the time I came home in the evening, she was in a pool of tears and emotionally exhausted. Jeanette, a busy toddler, was learning to talk, and Bert was learning to walk. They both still needed a lot of Freddie's attention.

Freddie needed rest. Her only relief was when Jeanette and Bert took naps, but even then Wallace and the housework took their toll on her. Her friends and family came to help as often as they could, but it was still hard.

The boys enjoyed their uncles, Louis and Charlie Bludorn, and were thrilled when they came to visit. Louis, however, was spending increasing amounts of time away in Iowa. Freddie had never visited them that I knew of, but her mother had many relatives in Davenport, Iowa. Louis was courting a girl there named Maude.

Charles still owned his land in Dakota Territory and worked as a seed salesman there. He had bought Louis' and his father's land and maintained the farm. Charles was married and had a daughter, also named Maude. Charlie traveled a lot and he came to visit in Chicago regularly, but his wife and daughter did not. In 1888, Anna (Charlie's wife) and their daughter moved to Missouri. Charlie was sad when he

received word that Anna had been pregnant when she left for Missouri, and the child, a little girl she named Myrtle, died that winter. Anna buried her in Mineral Springs cemetery. We weren't sure if Anna and Charles had marriage problems, but we did not ask.

During the last week of the fair, I worked at the Rueckheim's booth. One day a sudden commotion and panic overcame the huge crowds. The rumor was that someone had murdered the newly elected mayor of Chicago, Mr. Carter Harrison, Sr. I was not a United States citizen and so I never got involved with politics, but I knew that Mr. Harrison was well liked. It was October 28 and the fair was scheduled to close two days later on October 30. The news of the mayor's death brought everything to a halt, and the atmosphere of the fair changed immediately from joyful and happy to mournful and sad. Instead of a victorious closing ceremony, a funeral and memorial were being arranged. I later heard that the murderer was captured by the police and executed.

I helped pack up all the candy and close the booth. Louis gave me the name of a Mr. Wirth. He was a candy jobber and might be able to give me some work. Louis was able to recommend me as a friend and a successful salesman.

Soon after the fair's last day, I located Mr. Wirth and proposed my plan to him. If he could let me sell candy from his wagon during the day, then I could preach in the evenings and on weekends. I would be willing, eventually, to invest in his business and become a partner. He agreed to give it a try. As I talked with him, I asked him if he knew

the Lord Jesus as his Savior. I shared the scriptures with him and he became a believer as well.

Freddie and the children still needed me at home as much as possible. When I was there I helped do chores and care for the children. Although busier than ever, I had energy and felt very good. Freddie, on the other hand, did not feel well at all. By early summer we could no longer deny the obvious—she was again pregnant. Even the thought of six children, three of them under the age of five, was exhausting. I tried to stay home as much as possible, but I had to work to make ends meet. I prayed every morning, asking God to give Freddie and me strength for each day. As we collapsed into bed at night we thanked Him for meeting all our needs.

I still spoke at the Methodist church on Thursday nights, and Saturday and Sunday mornings. Many more Jewish people heard my testimony and the good news of God's salvation through Jesus. With the help of the Bletsch family and others from the church, the meetings were able to continue, and each week a few of my people came to know and love the One who suffered the punishment for our sins.

I put my Bible in the candy wagon each morning when I began work. If business was slow, I brought out that treasured book and read. I wanted so much to show my children the gospel in a way that they could easily remember. I had written papers while I was at Moody in which I discussed in detail the scriptures that outline God's plan of salvation, but I knew that God's love was simple enough that even children could understand and remember it. After all, our Lord loved

children and said, "Except ye be converted and become as little children, ye shall not enter into the kingdom of heaven. Whosoever therefore shall humble himself as this little child, the same is greatest in the kingdom of heaven" (Matt. 18:3-4). The songs and stories the children learned on Sunday morning were taking root in their hearts and minds, but maybe there was something, perhaps a picture, that would help them remember all that Jesus did for us.

I prayed that God would show me a simple message to share with the children—something that they could use to tell the story themselves.

Chapter Fourteen

Stripes!

We moved a few blocks away, to a larger house on the corner of Thirteenth and Hoyne. Freddie's energy rebounded a little, but she could not keep up with the demands of five children, much less six.

As I had thought, the candy business grew after the World's Fair, and Wirth and I worked out a good arrangement. I would work in the early morning hours and he would take over so I could be home to help Freddie when the boys came home from school. The house was always a beehive of activity. I had the choice of either watching the little ones or starting the preparations for supper. Freddie was a good mother, and she had determined to spend time with each child whenever they needed her. Our table at suppertime began with prayer, thanking God for all He had provided, and then we had a rendering of the day's events.

As the fall leaves fell and the cold winds of winter made us aware of the change in seasons, the obvious signs of a new life in Freddie's womb signaled a change in our family as well. Yes, there would be another mouth to feed, but the joy of a baby brother or sister excited all the children. Jeanette wanted a sister, but the boys were unsure whether another girl in the house would be good. Nettie, as her brothers called her, was enough, they thought. She couldn't play like the boys. She wanted to play with dolls, and she often got her own way. Since she was the only girl, Freddie made frilly little dresses for her. We treated her differently than the boys because she was a girl, but sometimes it appeared that we spoiled her. I made sure the boys protected their sister and treated her like a lady. Whether the new addition would be a boy or a girl, our lives would certainly need some adjustments.

For eight years, ever since I first received the wonderful gift of salvation, I had loved Christmas. The birth of God's Son was truly a reason for celebration. At Moody we learned that all of history was changed when God sent His own dear Son to earth to live among us. Freddie's family had always celebrated Christmas, but until I was saved, it meant nothing to me. With children, it became a wonderful season for our family. Our house was large enough to accommodate a big dinner. Freddie's father, brothers, aunts, uncles, and cousins were all welcomed, and of course we invited people who had nowhere else to go. Our home was full of food, laughter, and joy.

To begin with, the story of the birth of the Savior was read from the Holy Word for all to hear. Songs that proclaimed His birth were sung joyfully, and we even formed caroling parties so that our joy could spill over into the streets of the whole neighborhood. We gave each of the children one small gift, but the focus was on the birth of the Savior in Bethlehem long ago.

We knew that our new baby would come around Christmas this time. Freddie's birthday was on Christmas Day, and Frank's birthday was also in December, but there was just something special about a newborn baby at Christmastime. Freddie and I planned on opening our home again, but we knew that Freddie would have to sit this one out. I could cook the turkey and provide enough candies for all. The rest of the food would have to be prepared by others, since Freddie was confined to bed rest. She wanted to be a part of the hustle and bustle, but the doctor had warned her, and she knew her body was too weak.

Though uncomfortable, Freddie never let her smile fade. She was determined to enjoy Christmas. Friends and family helped with the other children and the daily housework.

Two weeks before Christmas, her pains started. I went for Dr. Bundesen and then took Jeanette and Bert to Christian's house. The older boys were at school. At that time, Freddie's father and Louis were living in a house on Dodson Street. I went by to tell Wirth that I would not be able to work, went to the school to advise the boys to walk to their grandfather's house after school, and then quickly went back home to check on Freddie. She was pale and in a lot of pain. I

was relieved when the doctor finally arrived. This had been a difficult pregnancy, and I was worried about Freddie and the baby. Dr. Bundesen was a new doctor, and I prayed that he would help Freddie and our child through this birth. All of our children, except for Carrie, had been born healthy and strong. Freddie had always been strong too, but this time seemed different. The hours dragged on and on. Finally, I heard the soft cry of the baby. Dr. Bundesen called me into the room and I met our seventh child, another boy. We named him George Albert. Baby George was small and seemed more fragile than the others had been. Freddie was tired, and Dr. Bundesen told me to let her sleep as much as possible. Her health would return, but it would take time.

The doctor wrapped George in a warm blue blanket and laid him in my arms. I thought about the Christmas story. I wondered how Joseph must have felt holding Jesus for the first time. I lifted my voice in prayer, thanking God for this new son. I had already been blessed beyond what I deserved. George slept quietly and peacefully.

I pondered how God sent His son to die in my place. How could God love me, a wretched sinner, enough to allow His perfect, blameless son to take the penalty for *my* sins? I could not imagine sacrificing any of my children.

When the children came home from Christian's house, they met their new brother. I kept George at a safe distance, because when he woke up it seemed he had trouble breathing. He wheezed and coughed. I was afraid for him. I sent word to Dr. Bundesen, and he

came back to check the baby. He said to keep the baby warm and call for him again if his breathing did not improve. Freddie slept for a long, long time. She woke up only long enough to sip some hot soup and to feed George. Many Bludorn relatives came to sit with Freddie and help her take care of the baby, and I was so thankful for their help. The rest of the children were my responsibility.

After a week's time, Freddie had grown stronger, and so had George. We watched the snow falling outside and tried to stay warm. Friends and family came to visit and they brought gifts for the new baby. Again I was reminded that kings and wise men from the east had brought gifts at Jesus' birth. Their gifts, however, were given to a newborn King, no ordinary baby. They were gold, frankincense, and myrrh—strange gifts, and costly, to be sure. The gifts we received were much more practical—diapers, talcum powder, and a rattle.

I loved all these teachable moments for my children, and God was creating, in my mind, the visual tool for which I had asked. I couldn't wait to get back to work.

On Friday, December 21, 1894, Freddie's aunts and cousins came to visit. They all took turns helping with baby George and caring for the older children. Jeanette played with her dolls. The boys helped decorate the house with red and green paper garlands, which they had learned to make at school. They baked cookies with their aunts and practiced singing their songs for caroling. I told Freddie that I needed to go to the candy wagon. I would try not to be gone long.

Wirth and I had designed a wagon together where our confections could not only be displayed, but also made. The wagon had a small cook stove, and I heated it up for my use that night. The stars shone overhead and yet another portion of the Christmas story came to life in my mind. How must the star have appeared to those shepherds in the field with their sheep? How bright the skies must have been, and how beautiful the angel choir must have sounded.

I looked at all the candies Wirth and I sold. So sweet for our customers, and yet, oh so much sweeter still is the gift of salvation from God who loves us so much. He didn't even spare His own son. *How can I tell them, Lord?* I looked up and saw the white peppermint stick candies displayed on the shelf above me. These were like the ones Freddie and Lizzie Berthold bought from me in front of the dress shop. I picked one up and paused. I turned it over and over in my hands. I wondered. I heated the stick until it was soft and pliable. On one end, I bent the stick upward. "There," I thought, "that looks like a letter 'J', just like the first letter in the name of Jesus." I prayed, "Lord, help me to see what You are telling me here."

Okay, what was it about this candy? When it cooled, the "J" was hard and white. Hard candy—Jesus. You are my rock, strong and always dependable. White—just like Jesus' purity. You, Jesus, are holy and sinless. Could this be a way to show the gospel? Through my candy? I took some red dyed peppermint candy and melted it in a small tin over the cook stove. When it was liquid, I dipped a small paintbrush in it. I drew a wide red line as I twirled the peppermint stick

in my fingers. Red—like Your precious blood that was shed, Jesus. Then I took an even smaller brush and painted three narrow stripes in the same way I had done the wide one. These are to represent Your crown of thorns, the wounds on Your hands and feet, and the cross where You died. As I finished, I realized that I could make these for all my children, but also for those who came to my Sunday morning meetings at Sunshine Mission. The message would be easy to remember.

Hard candy—Jesus is our Rock, strong and dependable.

White color—Jesus is the holy, sinless, and pure Son of God.

Peppermint flavor—like the gift of the Wise Men.

The letter "J"—for the name of Jesus.

Cane—Jesus is our Good Shepherd; shepherds use their staff to care for their sheep.

The color red—represents Jesus' blood that was shed for our sins.

Broad stripe—represents Jesus' sacrifice.

Three narrow stripes—the crown of thorns, the wounds on Jesus' hands and feet, and the cross.

I worked quickly and made all our peppermint sticks into "J" shapes and then painted stripes on them. It was still a few days until

Christmas, but I wanted to give them to the children on Sunday morning. I left them in the wagon and went home. The whole family was asleep when I walked back into the house. I didn't realize how long I had been gone, but the smell of cookies and the brightly decked halls told me the evening had been good.

I sat down and opened my Bible. In Isaiah 9:6 I read, "For unto us a child is born, unto us a Son is given." Then I turned again to Isaiah 53, "And by his stripes we are healed." How? How could that be? I prayed one last time before I dozed off. "I don't understand, but thank you Lord for healing us…for healing me."

Chapter Fifteen

Family Forgotten

The children at home and at the Sunshine Mission enjoyed the candy "canes" very much, and my heart was overjoyed when I heard them telling other children the gospel story as they shared their candy. It had been a wonderful Christmas.

Freddie and baby George were getting stronger every day, but George still seemed to get sick more than any of our other children. He seemed to have a cough and sniffles all the time. The doctor didn't think it was serious and said we just needed to keep him warm. He said he might outgrow it and be fine. As the doctor had predicted, Freddie regained her strength, but it was slow.

After Christmas, our home was blessed again by another addition. One of our Christmas guests, a fifteen-year-old orphan girl named Eva came to live with us.

When she had still been able to do her Christian work with Miss Dreyer, Freddie had met Eva and her mother in their small apartment a few blocks from Ashland Methodist Church. Freddie had taught Eva to sew and read the Bible to Eva's mother, who was very ill. When Freddie had to postpone her work because of her health, she worried that Eva would not be able to care for her mother without help. Miss Dreyer made sure that someone from the women's group continued to visit Eva and her mother, and she sometimes made those visits herself.

Eva had lived most of her life with only her mother. She did not remember her father at all and she knew of no other family. She barely remembered coming to Chicago from Minnesota. She couldn't remember what city they had lived in or why they left.

Her mother had encouraged Eva to attend the Saturday morning Bible study at the Methodist church, and although reluctant to leave her mother alone, Eva came regularly to those meetings. Wise beyond her years, she was a quick learner and always eager to help with the younger children.

Eva's mother became weaker and weaker. One day in early December, Eva came home to find that her mother had slipped into eternity with a smile on her face. Though sad to lose her, Eva was glad

that her mother's suffering had come to an end. She knew her mother was with Jesus and that someday she would see her again, but here on earth Eva found herself homeless and alone.

Eva came to our house every day to help with the Christmas preparations, and often she would sleep in Jeanette's room at night. She enjoyed our home and was a tremendous help to Freddie. Whenever an extra hand was needed to care for the baby or play with Nettie, Eva was there. She used her sewing skills to make clothes for the children, and each article was a work of art. Her stitches were precise, and her seams and hems were neat and even. She loved sewing and often worked late into the night.

Within a few days, Eva became a part of our family. We all loved her—even the boys—but Jeanette took Eva by the hand as often as possible and pulled her to the corner where her dolls and tea cups were always set up. Eva had attended school until she was twelve, so she was able to read and write. She read stories to the younger children and helped the older ones with schoolwork whenever she could.

Shortly after the New Year we found that a house just two doors from Christian's house on Dodson Street was available. We loved the house and immediately decided to move the family again. Being close to her father made Freddie happy. She could spend time with him every day and begin to take an active part in caring for him as he grew older. He was happy too, knowing that our family was nearby. The boys loved their grandpa and listened to his stories for hours. Christian loved to watch Nettie play because it reminded him of

happy days in Chippewa when Freddie was a little girl. He often said it was too bad Catherine could not enjoy the grandchildren with him.

With Eva in our home, I had time again to study the Bible intensively, accept invitations to speak and to write tracts. I corresponded with C. J., who had moved to Kansas City. I read accounts of the work there and asked him questions. The tent business was thriving and providing covers for hundreds of wagons headed west to places such as New Mexico, California, Oregon, and Oklahoma. C. J. had employed about 300 people. They held Bible meetings during lunch breaks and many of the workers were now believers. A congregation was assembling at a building they had secured on Main Street, which was just a dirt road. Several of the women had gathered street urchins and had begun Sunday school classes for children. After working at the shop all day, C. J. would then preach for two hours each evening. Over 150 people were in attendance at most of the meetings.

C. J. was interested in the book of Revelation and the scriptures about our eternal destinies and rewards. He was developing a new chart called "Life and Death." His chart "Two Roads and Two Destinies" was being printed onto large pieces of canvas that he would use in his preaching and teaching meetings.

I shared with him my concern for my Jewish family in Germany and explained that I wanted to tell them the gospel. Many Jewish people in Chicago had heard me and were baptized in the name of the Lord Jesus. Besides writing about my own personal experiences

with the Lord Jesus Christ, I wrote an extensive article addressing all the requirements I could find in scripture for Messiah and the scriptures that show Jesus fulfilled each one. There could be no doubt that Jesus was the One we had been waiting for.

One day I received a letter from Philadelphia from my brother Siegfried. My hands trembled as I opened the letter and read the words. Siegfried had come to the United States in 1884, married, and had three sons—David, Leon, and Sidney. I wept as I read the names, because I knew simply by seeing the name David that my father must have died. Jewish people name a child after a relative only after that person's death. In spite of this sad news, I was thrilled to hear from my brother. Siegfried was my closest sibling—just two years older than me. I prayed with Freddie and asked C. J. about it. We decided I should make a trip to Philadelphia to see Siegfried. Within a few weeks I had saved up enough money for a train ticket.

I telegraphed Siegfried to let him know I was coming to visit, then boarded the train. I had not been on a train since I had come to Chicago. The trip gave me long periods of time to pray and think about all the questions I had. Would my brother be happy to see me? How had he changed in all these years? Would he understand my faith in Jesus? Would he even listen? The time went by much faster than I had anticipated.

As I stepped off the train at the depot in Philadelphia, I recognized my brother immediately. Of course he was older, but he really hadn't changed that much from the sixteen-year-old I

remembered in Germany. He was dressed in a nice suit, more expensive than anything I had ever worn. Beside him was a beautiful dark-haired woman holding a child about the same age as George. As I approached my brother, he did not smile. He did not embrace me. There was only a cold empty space between us.

"Siegfried," I said, hoping the warmth I carried in my heart for him came out of my mouth.

"Hello," he said, and he took my small bag. He introduced me to his wife, Rosa, and son, Sidney. She seemed pleasant, but also did not extend the reception I had hoped for. We rode in a carriage to their home.

Siegfried told me that he was a salesman for fine men's clothing. His other children were at school, so we sat in the parlor and talked. Rosa took Sidney into the kitchen to make some refreshments. Siegfried said they had hoped to never hear from me again when I left home.

"Mutter cried for days and could not be consoled that her child was gone," he said.

I thought of my sorrow at losing Carrie, and now for the first time I could understand the pain my foolish rebellion had caused. Siegfried continued, "Papa would not even let us mention your name. You brought disgrace to the Kapp family, and we had to live with the shame of 'the rebel.' Being the rabbi in Hechtsheim, it was especially

hard for Papa, and finally, after a year or so, he left and we never saw him again. I received word last year that Mutter finally died without any hope of seeing you again." A long, uncomfortable silence followed. I could tell this was not the time to talk about my faith. Maybe in a few days there would be an opportunity.

David and Leon came home from school and Rosa served us some tea and pastries. I marveled at how Siegfried's children and mine had such similar facial features. I spoke of Freddie and of each of the children. Siegfried asked about the World's Fair and if we had seen the big wheel. I told him about all that we had seen, and also talked about Rueckheim's candy business.

After a wonderful dinner prepared by servants, Siegfried showed me to a guest bedroom upstairs. He said, "You must be tired from your long trip. We will talk again in the morning." My bag had been placed in this room, I supposed by a servant. The silence in this house was a stark contrast to the joyful noises and wonderful chaos in ours. I changed into my pajamas, lay down on the bed, and read from the Bible I had packed. I really was more tired than I had realized. I closed my precious book, and then my eyes. Just before I drifted off into sleep, I prayed, "Lord, give me the words to say tomorrow."

The next morning I heard footsteps and voices in the hallway. I thought it must be the children getting ready for school. I wondered when Siegfried would go to work, but he had said we would talk this morning. Maybe he would stay home today. It was Wednesday, Mitwoch, so it should be a school and work day. Soon I heard a knock

on the door. Siegfried announced that breakfast was being served. I dressed quickly and went downstairs to the dining room. Rosa, Siegfried, and all the children were seated at the table. All sorts of fruits and breads were displayed. Everything was kosher. A servant asked if I would like coffee, tea, milk, or juice to drink. I chose tea, and Siegfried prayed a Hebrew prayer of blessing. Again it seemed awkward because of the silence. After they had eaten, David and Leon asked to be excused. They stood up, went to their mother and gave her a kiss on the cheek, then told their father good-bye and left for school. Rosa stood up with Sidney in her arms and politely excused herself.

"It was nice to have met you," she said. I stood and nodded. After she left, Siegfried and I went to the parlor again.

"I believe it would be best if you go back to Chicago today. There is a train at noon," he said.

"What about us?"

Siegfried responded, "What do you mean? I once had a younger brother, but he has been gone for a long, long time. I do not know where he is now."

I wanted to shout, "I'm here," but restrained myself. Instead I said, "I want to tell you about the life I've discovered and the joy I've found."

"I am happy for you," he said curtly, and then left the room. I was so shocked and confused. A servant came in and asked if he could help with my bag.

"No," I said. Why had Siegfried allowed me to come? Was he just curious?

The train ride back to Chicago seemed extremely long. A whirlwind of emotions flooded me. Anger, hurt, disappointment—all of that, and more. But what did I expect? After all these years, why was I surprised at the cool reception? I thought of Joseph and his reunion in Egypt with his brothers after such a long time, and I wished my experience had a happier ending—but then, I had created my own problems, hadn't I? My brothers hadn't sold me and left me, although they might have felt like doing it. I had left them. How could I expect Siegfried to want to resume our boyhood friendship now as if nothing had ever happened? I had left home in anger and hadn't even cared who got hurt. *Oh Lord, please forgive me. I know You love me and You love them too. How can I tell them about You since I have treated them so badly? I am so sorry. Don't let me be a stumbling block to my family any longer. Don't let me keep them from finding You.* I opened my Bible and read from Romans 9:1-3 where Paul said, "I say the truth in Christ. I lie not. My conscience also bearing me witness in the Holy Ghost, that I have great heaviness and continual sorrow in my heart. For I could wish that myself were accursed from Christ for my brethren, my kinsmen according to the flesh." Yes, I understood what

Paul meant. I fell to sleep on the train, exhausted in body, mind, and soul.

When the train arrived in Chicago, it was late. I walked home and entered the house quietly. Freddie woke up and greeted me, surprised I had come home so soon.

"How did it go?" she asked softly, but she'd already seen the sadness on my face. I told her all that happened. I hugged her and sobbed uncontrollably for a long time. Finally, we prayed together. I knew she needed her rest so I told her to go back to bed. I just needed a little more time alone with my Savior.

Chapter Sixteen

Lake Forest

The sting of the visit with Siegfried never really went away. My heart was still tender when I thought of him, but I knew that until the Spirit worked in his heart, my words would be unwelcome.

Freddie and I were going to be parents for the eighth time. George was a toddler, and although we still called for a doctor now and then when he had trouble breathing, Freddie was healthy and strong. Eva was like a daughter to us, and with her help Freddie did not get as tired and weak during this pregnancy. Frank was thirteen, Edward was ten, and Wallace was eight. They went to school during the day. Frank and Edward were good students, but Wallace was often in trouble, and the principal and teachers frequently contacted us about his behavior. Nettie, age five, learned her alphabet and numbers with Eva's help. Bert was four and George was two. Freddie, Eva, and the

younger children loved going to the park, only a few blocks from our house. The older boys enjoyed being outdoors too. Frank and Wallace played stickball or dodge ball with other kids in the neighborhood. Edward preferred reading and drawing.

I worked as much as possible with the candy wagon. Wirth and I had a routine, and our sales were good. Studying, speaking, and writing took up the rest of my time. I loved God with all my heart and I knew He had blessed us more than we deserved.

Freddie was so hospitable that our home constantly buzzed with activity. With the children getting older, their friends often became dinner guests. Freddie and Eva planned birthday parties, baby showers, weddings, Christmas parties, anniversary parties, and all sorts of celebrations. Joy and peace reigned in our home for the most part, and it was fun for the children and for me.

In the spring of 1897 Paul Bludorn Capp was born. It seemed appropriate to finally name one of the children for Freddie's father. He had loved us and been near to us throughout all our married life. He had always been helpful and he never judged me, even though he had plenty of reasons to. I could see that Freddie had acquired many of his good, loving character traits, and I hoped some of our children would develop kind, tender hearts as well.

Christian grew weaker as the days went by. Louis had married and moved to Iowa with his wife. Charlie was in Dakota and Missouri, so he didn't visit his father as often as he used to. Freddie spent more

time with her dad, and every day she either took food to him, or he'd come to our house for dinner.

I shared with Freddie the letters from C. J. that were full of stories about the work in Kansas City. C. J.'s wife Eliza and their four daughters were active in the evangelism work as well as the tent and awning business. Hundreds of wagons headed west with families. Kansas City was the last place for these people to stock up with supplies. The trains also brought people west. The awning business and the congregation grew quickly.

Freddie and I talked about perhaps going to help out someday, but for now our family and work were here in Chicago. My meetings on Thursday nights and Saturdays still drew Jewish people to the Savior. I began by teaching from the book of Ezekiel and Isaiah and then presenting the life of Jesus. I watched as the Holy Spirit revealed to each one the true identity of Jesus. A glow came across each face when that recognition occurred. From that point on, people displayed an unquenchable thirst to learn more. Each week in the spring and summer I was asked to baptize several new believers. We went to a lake or beach and baptized each person by immersing them.

C. J. and I had discussed the fact that many Protestant denominations were baptizing by sprinkling water on the head, and yet as we read the scripture, that just didn't line up with the baptism practiced by the New Testament churches. In fact, many practices of the mainline denominations were points of contention with C. J., his friend Donald Ross, and others who had joined the Northern

Evangelistic Association. They studied scripture and taught a simple salvation message that was received and followed by a growing and devoted congregation in Kansas City.

I had never aligned with any one particular denomination except for when I had received the kindness of Jacob Bletsch and the Ashland Methodist Church for my meetings. I'd had invitations to speak at churches of many denominations to share the story of my personal salvation. Freddie's parents came from an Evangelical Lutheran background, but Christian did not seem offended by any of my teachings. My "non-denominational" stance and the fact that I was a Jewish man teaching about Jesus were very unique and unusual.

Wirth, my candy partner, had suggested that we move north. He knew of a community a short distance north of Chicago called Lake Forest where many wealthy people had built homes. So we took our candy wagon there. We found that our candy was popular with vacationers and residents. Lake Forest had beautiful parks, and the people there had time for leisure and games. They played golf and tennis and swam in crystal-clear swimming pools.

One of my favorite customers was the editor of the local newspaper. The Lake Forester was published once a week. The editor had heard me speak and wondered if I would be interested in writing a column. It was an exciting proposition, but I doubted that I could find the time to do it every week. I told him I would pray about it and give him an answer soon. I went home and told Freddie about the offer. The extra income would help meet our family's needs. We decided that I

would remain anonymous, though, so that only God would get the glory. But what could I write?

In my personal Bible study I had been reading through the book of Proverbs. The wisdom of Solomon and the contrasts he made in his writing fascinated me. He used short statements with gems of truth woven into common sayings. I sat down at my desk and jotted down some thoughts. Some of the words that came from my pen that day were, "adversity is often a blessing," "patience is power," "theology may change but the gospel does not," "we will only love to live when we live to love," "true religion may find its dining table in the church, but its workshop will be in the word," and "there can be no peace in the heart while we are fighting against the will of God." On and on I wrote. Would this make any sense in a newspaper article? I decided to entitle the column "Ram's Horn Blasts—Warning Notes Calling the Wicked to Repentance." I took my ideas to Lake Forest the next day and showed them to the

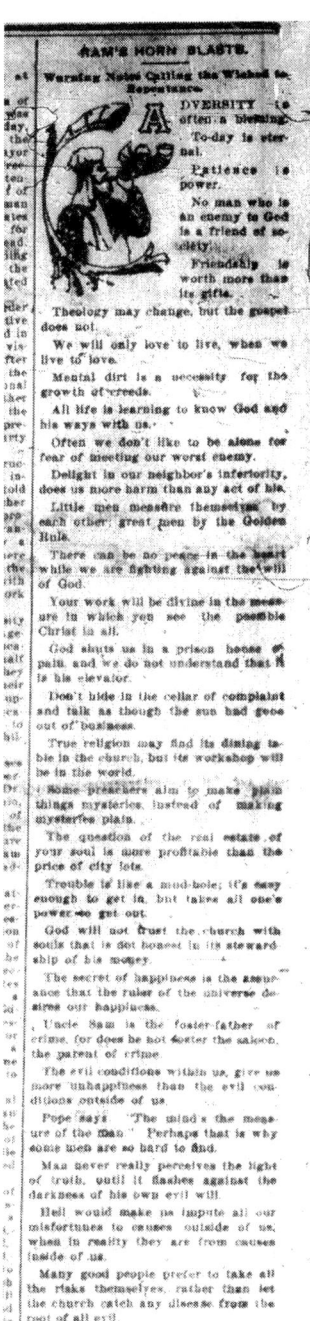

Ram's Horn Blast
July 1, 1899

editor. I was amazed that he liked them.

"Can we add a picture of a priest blowing the ram's horn?" he asked. I agreed, and the next week, July 15, 1899, he printed the first installment of my column. It was well received and people asked him who wrote it. He respected my request to remain anonymous and did not tell or print my name. It was August fifth before my next entry.

The last week of August I was asked to speak at Fort Sheridan. The large audience consisted mostly of soldiers. They listened attentively, and many came to faith that day. I was thrilled that men who may be going to battle soon had found peace with God through the Lord Jesus Christ. I thought that someday my own boys might join the army, and I would not want their eternal destinations unsettled then.

Week after week I traveled to Lake Forest and left Freddie and the family in Chicago. We decided it was time to move to Lake Forest. We knew we could not leave Christian alone, so we hunted for a house that would accommodate our family, including Eva and Christian. In October we found that a large house owned by Miss Materson had become available. Freddie and I traveled to Depot Avenue to see the house. It seemed to meet all our needs. It was spacious and had plenty of room for entertaining, as Freddie and Eva both liked to do. The only problem was its close proximity to the railroad tracks. Every day and night several trains passed through Lake Forest, and the rumbling and whistle blowing was something to which we would all have to grow accustomed. We were especially concerned about Christian, who was

nearly eighty-four years old, as well as the new baby Freddie was carrying.

Oh yes, we were now expecting again. With Freddie now well into her forties, I found myself worried for several reasons—the difficulties she'd had with previous pregnancies, the move, caring for her elderly father, and now the added work of the coming holidays. Could she carry this baby and deliver it without problems? Her doctor was so far from our new home. Again, Eva stepped in and was a tremendous help. I loved Freddie and wondered selfishly how I would manage our household without her should the Lord take her home with this birth.

The move went smoothly. We were able to use the train to our advantage. The whole family stepped off the train, walked a short distance, and arrived at the front door of our new house. Our belongings had been transported in the freight part of the train and unloaded at the dock, and then our boys and I were able to take them to the house. The boys loved the trains and watched them come and go, taking people and cargo to faraway places. Nettie loved to see ladies in fine clothes get off the train for vacations in Lake Forest. We gradually got used to the low rumble and to the whistles announcing their arrivals and departures.

In December I spoke for the first time at the Gospel Hall, which was owned by a Mr. Healy. The newspaper announced it like this: "At the Gospel Hall, Sunday, December 17, M. Capp will give his life history and how he became a Christian, being a Jew by birth.

Come and hear his reason why the gospel of Christ is the power of God unto Salvation. You are welcome."

I had to give up my meetings at Ashland Methodist Church and Sunbeam Mission when we moved, but I saw God leading me and our family in a new direction. I couldn't help but wonder if anyone would make the connection between me and the "Ram's Horn Blasts" column. I guessed it didn't matter, but I still preferred to remain anonymous as much as possible. After all, the gospel message was not about me, but about the Lord Jesus Christ and His gift of salvation from sin. I hoped the people of Lake Forest would receive it.

They did. Week by week, the Lord gave me words for the newspaper column and for the messages at the Gospel Hall.

The Christmas holiday, however, was a gala affair in Lake Forest. There was a party atmosphere, but little worship of the newborn King. I saw that the gospel message was overshadowed by the desire for pleasure and comfort here. There was much work to be done.

One cold January morning Freddie went into labor. It was too early for the baby, and I was panicked. I did not know of any doctors in Lake Forest. While she stayed with Freddie, Eva sent me to notify a woman from the church. Maybe she would know of a doctor or midwife. While I was gone, Freddie's pains increased and the baby was born. He was small and blue. Eva wrapped him and tried to bring life into him, but it was too late. When I came back with a local doctor,

there was nothing he could do. I knelt down next to the bed and prayed with Freddie for our son. We named him Leon. The people from the Gospel Hall were kind, and helped us to find a burial plot in the Lake Forest cemetery. The other children were confused and sad about the events of that day, but they busied themselves by playing in the snow. It gave their mother and me time to mourn.

Freddie was back to her normal self physically within a few days, but she knew this baby would be her last, and the sadness lingered for months. The reality of a sick father and a house full of children soon required her attention, so she trusted the Lord that even this, another lost child, would work together for good.

The Lord seemed to be leading me to teach a series of Bible readings about Jesus' soon return. Perhaps these messages were spurred on by my interest in C. J.'s charts and tracts. The newspaper faithfully published the topics and information about the Gospel Hall meetings, and each week the numbers grew.

The children loved living in Lake Forest. They made friends and enjoyed the sports and games. Frank, who was sixteen, wanted to take a job as a golf caddy. Freddie and I had no idea what a golf caddy was. We had watched men playing the game, which involved hitting a small ball with different clubs. It seemed the goal was to get the ball into a small hole a long distance away. Frank explained that his job would be to carry the bag with all the clubs and follow the player to the ball. That seemed like a simple enough job, and as long as he kept his studies and chores done, we told him he could work. Frank brought

home some balls and the younger boys enjoyed playing their own version of golf in our yard.

The house had a large porch where Christian enjoyed sitting in the sunshine and watching grandchildren. We knew that he was not well. Freddie sat with him for hours, nursing him in any way she could. After we had been in Lake Forest almost a year, a Swedish Lutheran man named J. A. Edlund came to the Gospel Hall. The services were similar to those Christian and Catherine had attended in their youth, and he enjoyed it very much.

Christian would sometimes share sayings and bits of wisdom, and he gave me permission to use them in the Horn Blasts. I, too, spent many pleasant evenings with Christian on that front porch.

After a year at the Gospel Hall we moved the meetings to Mrs. Green's house, near the West school where the children attended. Mr. Healey wanted to use his Hall for dances and entertainment. The use of his property was his decision, but it saddened me that we could no longer use his building to spread the "good news."

As winter approached again, Christian's breathing became more difficult. Freddie, Eva, and I knew the time was short. He no longer played with the children, and he slept more and more. One day Freddie went into his room to check on him around five o'clock in the morning and found that he had slipped away to heaven in his sleep. We were sad, and yet his death was not unexpected. We knew he was in the presence of the Lord we loved. Freddie notified her brothers, but

neither was able to come. We held funeral services for him the next day at our house. Two Lutheran pastors, Mr. Lancaster and Mr. Hopkins, came on the train from Chicago to officiate. We buried Christian in Lake Forest cemetery next to our son Leon.

Again we faced the holidays with sadness in our hearts. God had always been faithful to us though, and we knew He would bring joy into our lives again. If only we had known the changes that were to come.

Chapter Seventeen

Kansas City

After Christian's death we felt increasingly like God was leading us to Kansas City and the work started by C. J. Baker and others. Each letter from C. J. told of the need for the gospel in the cow town that was called Kansas City. Also, the tent and awning business was busily equipping the wagons taking families to the west, so there were opportunities to share the gospel as people passed through. It took a couple of years, but in June of 1903 I left the candy wagon to Wirth and we were all ready. All of us, that is, except Edward.

Edward would turn seventeen within a month, and he, like his brother, wanted to make his own money at the golf club in Lake Forest. He did not have the same outgoing personality as Frank, but he was kind, and people liked him very much. It was a hard decision, especially for his mother, but we allowed him to stay in Lake Forest

with another family as long as he paid them for his keep. I was concerned that the pleasures of the world would consume Edward's heart, but I also knew he was well grounded in the Word of God. Freddie and I prayed and then left Edward in God's hands as we boarded the train with the rest of the family.

Frank, nearly twenty, was anxious to see the tent and awning shop. He hoped that Mr. Baker would have a job for him. The only job he had held was his caddy job in Lake Forest, but as he walked with people and suggested which club they could use, he had developed people skills. He was naturally outgoing, friendly, and a good listener. We saw in Frank the potential to be a good leader. We knew it wouldn't be long before C. J. would see that potential as well and hire him.

Wallace, fifteen, was not all that happy about leaving Lake Forest. He had friends there and didn't understand why Edward got to stay and he didn't. Freddie and I gave him no choice about the matter, though. We knew he was too young and immature to be left without our daily discipline. As we traveled, his attitude changed a little. Seeing the wide open prairie and anticipating the adventure ahead gave him hope that this move wasn't as bad as it seemed at first, but he still didn't like being told he had to go with us. I understood. At his age I would have felt the same way.

Nettie also hated to leave Lake Forest and her friends. She was only twelve, and a girl, and Freddie and I were unsure whether this was going to be good for her. Freddie remembered how her parents

had left her in Chicago with her aunt and uncle when they moved west. It had been a good decision then, but we decided Nettie would be better off with us. Nettie had an adventuresome spirit that overcame her sadness at leaving. She vowed to write to her friends as often as possible and told them maybe she could return to visit sometime.

Eva was coming with us and she was excited, too. She and Nettie had become close friends and they chatted away the hours, talking and imagining the new places they would see and the new people they might meet. Like a big sister, Eva gave Nettie wise advice and helped her learn how to behave like a lady. The thought of leaving Eva in Lake Forest never crossed our minds. She was part of the family.

From the front porch of our house the kids had seen the powerful engines and cars of a train up close, but except for the short trip from Chicago to Lake Forest, they had no experience as passengers. Little did we know that this trip would be the first of many for them.

Bert, George, and Paul all watched out the window of the train as we passed mile after mile of prairie and farmland. When we stopped at towns along the way, they would watch people get on or off the train. Often loved ones stood on the platform giving final hugs or kisses, with tearful reunions or departures. This was a familiar sight for our children, but at every stop they would ask, "Are we there yet?" They were impatient to see the city we had talked about for so long. I hoped they wouldn't be too disappointed when we finally arrived.

Freddie and I couldn't fully picture what it would be like, so how could we answer their many questions?

Eating and sleeping on the train was a new experience for them, too. We had packed some food for the trip, so as evening approached we passed the basket around, said grace, and ate. The children had a lot of fun climbing up into the dormers and I wasn't sure they would ever quiet down, but the rocking of the train and the exhaustion of the day finally won, and soon they were sound asleep. Freddie, Frank, Eva and I stayed awake and talked for a while, sharing our hopes and dreams. Eventually sleep overcame even the adults, except for me. I opened my Bible and read about Abraham leaving his home in Ur to a land God would show him. As I drifted off into sleep I thanked God that He was with my family and me as the train carried us far away from our familiar home in Lake Forest.

I woke up before dawn and realized the train had stopped. Though still dark outside, my eyes adjusted and I looked out the window. The engineer, conductor, and a railroad employee stood on the platform. I strained to hear the conversation. Something seemed to be wrong, but none of them appeared panicked. They disappeared toward the front of the train. I waited for what seemed like an eternity. Passengers slowly roused and started asking what was happening, but we had to wait even longer for an answer. With the sun's first light, we couldn't believe what we saw. The train station platform at Alton, Illinois, looked like a boat dock. The waters of the Mississippi River had risen and the tracks ahead were underwater. The conductor came

inside and informed us that we would be loaded onto boats to cross the river. One of the railroad employees would go with us to direct us to another train on the other side of the huge river.

Freddie and I gathered up all the children and our bags. Each child had a bag, but we had packed lightly so that even Paul, the smallest, could carry his own. The conductor guided us to the gangplank of the steamship named *Bald Eagle* and we boarded. It looked like a sturdy vessel, but it was hard to see the other side of the swollen river and the current ran fast. We had to go underneath a bridge, and the river was so high that the *Bald Eagle* barely fit under it. The boys thought this was a great adventure, but Freddie and the girls shook with fear. About thirty minutes later the ship docked at the St. Louis train depot. The conductor accompanied our group of passengers to the train and took a head count to make sure everyone was accounted for. A few minutes later we were again on our way to Kansas City.

As we traveled we saw that the Missouri River was also flooded, but the railroad tracks were fine until we arrived at Slater, Missouri. It was obvious that repairs had been made recently on a section of the track there. We were told that the first train had crossed the new track just that morning.

As we approached Kansas City, the floodwaters were again widespread, and the conductor said we would not be able to depart the train at the Union Depot because it was six feet underwater. Instead, we got off the train several blocks away from the station. I wondered

how we would find C. J. and our other friends, but soon I saw a large wagon with the words "Baker-Lockwood Tent and Awning" on the side. I knew C. J. must be near.

Freddie and I rounded up the kids and luggage and searched the crowd for our friends from Chicago. It had been several years since we had seen them, but we finally spotted C. J., Eliza, and their daughters. We all started talking at once and for a long time all enjoyed the joyous confusion and laughter.

C. J. led us to the wagon. We traveled down the road away from the train station and the flood. The recent heavy rains had made everything muddy. The houses were simple wood frame buildings. So far, Kansas City did not look at all like the nicely kept drives and beautifully manicured estates in Lake Forest.

We stopped in front of a building, and C. J. announced that the upstairs floor was where the meetings were being held. We got out of the wagon and went to see the room. A group of ladies inside were teaching Bible stories to children who were dirty and barefoot. C. J. later explained that there were many orphans on the streets, and the ladies helped to meet both their physical and spiritual needs.

"As you can imagine," he said, "with the flood our work is even more crucial. There are so many people displaced from their homes and overwhelmed with need. It kind of reminds me of the desperate people in Chicago after the fire. As you know, they also are

in desperate need of a Savior for their souls. The harvest is plentiful, but the workers are few. Thank you for coming."

C.J. worked at the shop all day, and after a quick meal, he'd spend several more hours every night preaching the Gospel to those who came. He said he usually had fifty to one hundred people.

Eliza added, "It's wearing him out." I knew at that instant that this is exactly where God wanted us.

"I could preach and teach some classes for you," I said.

"Exactly what I was hoping you'd say," C. J. replied. "Let's get your family settled in and then we can talk."

Eliza and the girls took Freddie and the kids to an apartment down the street, and C. J. took Frank and me to the shop. The apartment was intended for visiting speakers and missionaries, not for a family of nine. It was very small, but we knew it would be a temporary home for us. There were two bedrooms and a small kitchen and living room. The boys could sleep on blankets on the hardwood floor, Eva and Nettie could sleep in one of the bedrooms, and Freddie and I would sleep in the other. We were thankful to have a roof over our heads. There were so many that didn't have even that much.

Chapter Eighteen

Work to be Done

We were all tired, and sleeping in the cramped apartment was difficult. The train had been more comfortable than this. The air was hot and humid. I thought of all the people whose homes and businesses were unusable due to the floodwater. We prayed that God would show us where to begin. We had nothing to offer other than our prayers and hands, and yet the next day we jumped head first into the work.

At the shop, C. J. had shown Frank and me all the different kinds of wagon covers, tents, cots, and awnings that they were able to make. As they had done in Chicago, C. J. and his employees gave tents to displaced people for shelter and provided cots for them to sleep on. We met many of the employees, and some were familiar faces from Chicago. It seemed that a person's ability in sewing or business was

not nearly as important to C. J. as their ability to share the gospel. He figured he could teach them to sew.

The machines ran long hours during this time of crisis, yet we found time during lunch breaks to read and share Bible teachings. The employees seemed happy and found joy in their work. C. J. put us to work right away. We cut, assembled, and folded canvas—we left the sewing to the ladies—and even Wallace and Bert were able to help. Occasionally we went out to set up the tents and cots for rescue shelters. C. J. supervised everything. Freddie, Eva, and Jeanette went with Eliza to the streets where people were looking for food, clothing, and a place to stay until they could return home. C. J. and Eliza had a nice house where hot meals could be prepared. The food was then distributed at the rescue tents and to the shop. In the evening, although we were all tired, we held gospel meetings in the upstairs room for a couple of hours. Many people were saved at those meetings. We often lingered late into the night talking to people, then we'd catch a few hours of sleep before starting again the next morning.

C. J. never seemed to stop. Sometimes employees would ask him if we could take a rest. His answer was that there would be plenty of rest in heaven; we need to be working down here. And so the work continued. Besides the flood relief, the shop was outfitting hundreds of wagons each week. Sometimes the line of wagons waiting to be equipped with a canvas cover would be a block or two long.

Either over dinner or while we were working, we learned more about the Baker family. C. J.'s oldest daughter, Maggie, had married

Robert Kerr in Chicago. His family owned a business that made canning jars. The Kerr's' business was miraculously saved during the great fire, much like C. J.'s tent business had been, and they gave God the glory. Maggie and Robert had come to Kansas City to scout out a place for the shop and the meetings. They were young newlyweds and worked hard, but they desired to return to Chicago.

Eliza's daughter, Grace Roe, married George Telfer. George's father was Robert Telfer, a well-known teacher for the Plymouth Brethren in Canada. Freddie was very interested since she was from Canada too. We met George in the shop, but he was not very friendly. George and Grace talked about owning their own business someday and moving west.

George's sister, Mrs. Rendall, was a wonderful teacher. All of our children loved her and enjoyed her Sunday school classes. When we held gospel meetings on the streets Mrs. Rendall was always present, leading the meeting with her beautiful singing. Frank used his baritone voice to praise God in our meetings, too. Music became a big part of our worship, and the beautiful sounds attracted crowds. Many people were brought into a relationship with the Savior—on the street, in the lunchroom, and in the nightly meetings in the upstairs room over Wolferman's Grocery Store. One curious visitor was a Catholic priest named Father Dalton. C. J. became a close friend to Father Dalton. Knowing that some of the Catholic teachings were not biblical, C. J. asked him why he stayed in a church with false teachings. Father Dalton said, "But what I teach is true, and what will happen to these

people if I leave?" He said he came to our meetings so that others seeing him would know that it was okay for them to listen to our messages, too.

C. J. and Eliza's second daughter, Jessie, had been married only a couple of years to a young man name William Sommerville. William was full of energy, much like C. J. Jessie had a small baby who was also named William, and was pregnant again. Her baby was due in August. She didn't do any of the heavy work; instead, she taught Bible stories to the street children.

A bright young man named Walter Wilson was a great asset to the gospel meetings. He was a medical doctor and very interesting. He wrote stories and children's books that explained God's wonderful creation from a scientific viewpoint. Walter and C. J. discussed the tabernacle in the heavens for hours; the way God designed plants to thrive in different climates, the way birds fly, and a multitude of other topics—always using scripture as a foundation, and connecting each story to the gospel story.

C. J. hired Walter to work in the shop. Walter became the doctor for all of the employees and was especially fond of C. J.'s daughter Marion. Plans were being made for them to get married the next year. Everyone loved Walter.

By late fall the work in the shop slowed down a little as people made progress cleaning and rebuilding their flooded homes and businesses. In our spare time we cut large pieces of canvas and Bible

verses were carefully printed on them. The banners were hung on the walls of the shop so that the employees and customers could see them. C. J. also had his chart "The Two Roads and the Two Destinies" printed in four colors on canvas for gospel meetings.

Freddie and I knew that we needed to get settled into a permanent home before school started. Our children had not been in school since March, and they would have some catching up to do in their studies. It wasn't until November that a house became available that was suitable for our family. Across the river in Kansas, its address was 2407 Fourth Street. A school sat across the street. We moved in, enrolled the kids in school, and prepared for our first Christmas in our new home. Since we had left everything but the bare essentials in Lake Forest, we had to find beds, tables, chairs, and all the household goods. C. J. let us keep the cots made at Baker-Lockwood that our kids had used as beds in the apartment. Freddie and Eva shopped while the children were in school, but since they had to take the trolley or walk, they were limited by how much they could carry. With their skill at homemaking, the house in Kansas looked warm and inviting in no time.

Wallace, Jeanette, Bert, and George were all in school, but little Paul would have to wait another year. He was too young. Frank was working for C. J. full time as a salesman. Circus troupes were purchasing tents for their shows, and C. J. measured and ordered according to the specifications they needed. He met the Ringling brothers and P. T. Barnum. There were strange sights, sounds, smells,

and people, but every day was exciting for him. His younger brothers and sister could hardly wait to hear the stories he told at dinner every night. It brought back memories of the World's Fair in Chicago.

At Christmas, C. J., Eliza, and their family were our guests. We were so thankful for dear friends who had helped us so much. We made candy canes, of course, and told the gospel story through the stripes to new children in a new place.

C. J. and I had time for some long discussions about the Gospel work in Kansas City. "Do you remember the conference in Chicago?" he asked me. I told him I did. "I think we should host a conference here in Kansas City. It could be at Christmas next year." It seemed like a far-fetched idea to me, but when C.J. had an idea it was difficult to change his mind. I could tell he was already working on the details for a Kansas City conference. "One thing is for sure, though," he said. "We won't allow any quarreling here. If any preacher wants to preach against some other preacher or against some assembly, or if he wants to find fault, he can go somewhere else to do it, but not here." I listened for hours, and C. J.'s ideas began to grow inside me, too.

Another conversation we had concerned my calling. I felt like my life and being a Jew who received Jesus as my Savior could be the basis for preaching the Gospel in tent meetings. People would think it odd, but I could show them that God's salvation is for all men, no matter who they were, how bad they were, or how bad they'd been in the past. I believed the railroad was the means to spread the gospel to small towns throughout the area. C. J. agreed. He told me to let him

know when and where God led me to preach. He would provide a tent and ten train tickets. The cargo fee for the tent was seven tickets, and the rest were for me and two others. We could set up the tent and advertise my meetings on posters and in the local newspapers. We would sleep in the tent or accept the hospitality of the local people. When the work was done, we would return to Kansas City by train. Freddie would be left at home alone with the kids for long periods of time, but she knew and accepted that this was what God wanted me to do. I would lift her burden as much as possible on the days I was home. We agreed that I would start in the spring. Freddie and I prayed and looked forward to this new chapter in our lives.

As the evening came to an end, Freddie read a letter and Christmas card that had arrived from Edward. The whole family sat in a circle and absorbed the precious words of love. We all missed him so much.

Paul, Jeannette, George and Bert

Chapter Nineteen

Edward

With spring right around the corner, Freddie and I prayed and talked about the plans C. J. and I had made. The children were all doing well in school, even Wallace. They did their chores and obeyed their mother.

C. J. had taught me and two of his employees how to raise the tent and secure all the ropes and poles. I had spoken at the Kansas City meetings on a regular basis, but this new adventure still gave me butterflies in my stomach. I would be speaking to people I'd never met before and who might even be hostile. I trusted God, though, and I knew that He would go before me.

The second week of March, George Telfer, William Sommerville, and I boarded a southbound train with tickets to a small

town called Peculiar, Missouri. Peculiar was an unusual name, but I believed God had directed me there. We arrived in the early afternoon on Monday, March 14. We set up the tent and went through the town putting up posters about the meetings. "Come and hear a Jewish man who talks about Jesus," the posters read. The first meeting was scheduled for the next afternoon. We had no lights, so our meetings had to end before dark. The farmers were getting ready for planting season, but the nighttime temperatures were still cold. I spoke on Tuesday, Wednesday, and Thursday. New people came each day and several gave their lives to the Savior. We were able to sleep in a barn near the edge of town. Several more accepted the gift of salvation there and we were filled with joy. We packed up the tent on Friday and caught the northbound train back to Kansas City.

When I got home, I shared with my family how God had used me. Freddie had kept everything in order at home, but she was glad that I was back. The next trip would require me to go farther and be gone longer, but for a while I studied the Bible, counseled people from the Kansas City congregation, spoke to people on the street or at C. J.'s shop, wrote letters, and helped Freddie with the housework.

There was a congregation in Belleville, Kansas that wanted me to come, so I bought train tickets for April 6. Freddie was concerned because we hadn't heard from Edward for several weeks. I told her he was probably fine, but if he hadn't written by the time I came home we would telegraph Lake Forest. I kissed everyone good-bye again and left for the train station.

We arrived in Belleville and set up the tent outside of town. The meetings had gone well for four or five days, and then I received a telegraph from Freddie. She told me that she had received word from Lake Forest that Edward had pneumonia. I immediately telegraphed our Chicago friends and asked how he was getting along. The hospital authorities replied that he would be released the next day, so I was not the least bit worried. I wrote back to Freddie and told her to send him money for the trip home as soon as he was strong enough.

Both Edward and I came home on the same day one week later, on April 18. Neither of us knew that the other would be coming at that time. He seemed to feel very well.

Freddie had wanted to make a trip to Mineral Springs, Missouri. She wanted to visit her brother, Charlie Bludorn, and his family, but wasn't sure if this was a good time. I reassured her that I could take care of the children and that she deserved a break. Edward was fine, and she could spend all the time she wanted with him when she returned. The evening before she left, Edward seemed to have a cold, but neither of us thought there was any danger. So on April 25 she went on her trip.

I had Edward sleep in the same room with me that night. I spoke to him very earnestly through the whole night, as the boy was unsaved. I showed him what an awful condition he was in and that if he had died in Lake Forest he would have been lost forever. Two days later he was still sick and never got up during the whole day. I called in a doctor that morning. The doctor said he might have only a cold,

but if it should prove to be a relapse of the pneumonia, I should get the nearest doctor as soon as possible.

Thursday afternoon a lady came to the house wanting to talk about the things of God. I was attending to the boy when she came, but went downstairs to talk with her. She left after about thirty minutes and I went back upstairs to check on Ed. He seemed to be resting so I returned downstairs to do some work. About four o'clock p.m. I went up again. He opened his eyes but soon became unresponsive. I telegraphed his mother to come home at once and sent for a doctor. Ed raved all night until four o'clock in the morning. After not recognizing me all night, he looked up and said, "That is papa." He then continued, "Pa, before I went to sleep, when the school was out (we lived across the street from the school) God saved my soul. Pa, if I had died in Lake Forest, I would be in hell now, but God in grace let me come home that he might save my soul."

Mrs. Warden, one of our neighbors, came in later that morning and the first thing Edward said to her was, "I am now a child of God." About three in the afternoon his fever rose very high. His skin was burning and he said to me, "Pa, I may become unconscious again."

"Ed, let us lay hold on God," I said. I knelt down by the side of his bed and prayed to God for Jesus' sake to not let him become unconscious again. Then he prayed, and out of all prayers I had ever heard, never had I heard anything like it. The essence of his prayer was, "Oh Father, for Jesus' sake do not let me get unconscious any more. Lord Jesus, Lord Jesus! Oh Lord Jesus do not let me get

unconscious." Immediately, his skin seemed to be more normal, but he still had a very high fever. From that moment on he remained awake.

The next morning was a Saturday. An eighty-three-year-old gentleman came to the house. Ed spoke to him and told him about the things of God, urging the old man to believe on the Lord Jesus. The old man, believing that Ed was dying, broke down and went away weeping. Ed asked me not to tell his mother about his salvation. He wanted to tell her first. He told every person that came in about the things of God. Again and again he called me to his bedside and asked me about certain things in the word of God. We always read the Bible morning and evening at our home, and when I went upstairs Saturday morning he asked me to read, so I read the sixth chapter of John. Some of the phrases in this section were, "Jesus, the bread of life; I will give you eternal life; they shall never perish; I will raise them up at the last day." When some of these statements were made, Ed said, "Pa, how sweet. Eternal life; never perish; raised the last day…" He lifted up his eyes toward heaven and thanked God for the Lord Jesus. He hugged me around the neck and kissed me, repeating that he was so thankful God did not let him die in Lake Forest but had brought him home so that he would be saved. After our Bible reading and praying, Edward laid hold on God for the salvation of every one of his five brothers and his sister. He wanted desperately for all of them to be saved. At one point he said, "Pa, I mistreated you, forgive me."

He waited all night and the next day for his mother to come home, but what we didn't know was that she never received the

telegram. So he never got to see her again. During the night he had fearful pains, as pleurisy had set in. Sunday morning, after reading the Bible, I knelt down by the side of his bed and prayed. Then he laid hold on God and said, "Father, if I have to die, let at least six or seven be saved through my death."

When the doctor came, he said the boy must be given some milk and whiskey. At once I sent for the whiskey to give him as the doctor had prescribed. The doctor said if Ed could cough up the phlegm his life might be saved. When he first tasted the whiskey he said to me, "Pa, I do not want to drink any whiskey—I have never tasted it before." But I said that the doctor told me that was the only way to preserve his life, so he said, "For your sake I will do it."

The boy continued to fail. I wanted to do all that was in my power to save the boy's life, but I could not take hold of God to restore the boy to health. I had no liberty in asking God to do so. I thought from the beginning that he was dying. But I did lay hold on God that he might make him a bright testimony.

About two o'clock in the afternoon the children went to Sunday school. Our Nettie, who was thirteen years old, did not go until about a quarter to three. Before she started I asked her if she did not want to see Ed before she went. When she came to him he put his arms around her and said, "Nettie, do believe on the Lord Jesus. Tomorrow by this time I might be in heaven. I want you to come there too, but you must believe on the Lord Jesus."

Nettie went away and left Ed and me in the house alone. I was kneeling down before God when Ed called me. He took me around the neck and sang, "Jesus Lover of My Soul." It was the sweetest thing I had ever heard. Again and again he repeated the phrase, "Jesus lover of my soul, Let me to Thy bosom fly."

Then many people came in. The death rattle was in his throat. I asked him once if he knew me. He smiled and said, "Yes, Pa, but I know Jesus better."

The children came home and went to the bedside weeping. They knew he was dying. Ed took each of them around the neck, kissed them, and told them to believe on the Lord Jesus and to meet him in heaven. It was the grandest sight. One after the other he urged them to believe on the Son of God. I knew there would only be a few more minutes, so I asked him again if he knew me. No reply. I asked him if he knew Jesus. He opened his eyes wide and made an effort to speak so that everyone in the room could understand that he recognized Jesus. He was passing into eternity at that very moment with the sweet name of Jesus on his lips.

At once there was a solemnity of God's presence in the room. Sweet peace came over my son. There were some fifteen people present, most of whom exclaimed, "What peace! What peace!" He smiled and his spirit went home to Jesus without a struggle, conscious and rational to the last.

After it was all over and Ed had passed away I entered the adjoining room, thanking and praising God for what I had seen. Surely, I thought, goodness and mercy have been following me all the days of my life. I prayed that Ed's request for his death to lead many others to the knowledge of the Lord Jesus, including his siblings, would be answered.

I knew that preparing for a funeral would be difficult, and I didn't know how I would find the strength. I also knew that first I had to contact Freddie. Tears ran down my face as I wrote the words for another telegram. "My dearest Freddie, our son has died. Please come home."

Freddie arrived home the next day. She blamed herself, she blamed me, and she questioned God. It was so difficult. I told her about his salvation, and his prayer for all his siblings to be saved. It comforted her to know that other people's lives would be changed forever because of Edward's testimony.

C. J. spoke at the funeral, and with sad hearts we buried Edward at Memorial Park Gardens.

Edward Capp

Age 16 Christmas 1902

Chapter Twenty

Moving On

It was a long time before Freddie could find peace about Ed's death. He was not the first child she had lost, but the others had been babies. This time she felt like she had abandoned her son when he needed her most. She questioned over and over whether he would have lived had she stayed home instead of taking the trip. She was angry that the first telegram did not reach her in time. Crushed and with all her strength gone, she did not eat and wanted to stay in bed. It broke my heart to see her grieve so much, but I could not help her. I wished she could have seen the peace on Edward's face as he entered the presence of our Lord. But through much prayer and time alone with God, Freddie finally regained her joy. Within a few weeks she was able to resume her work at home and at the church. The empty hole in her heart was being filled.

Jeanette was the first of the children to trust in the Lord Jesus. She told Freddie about Edward's plea for her to give her life to Jesus so she could go to heaven too. Nettie had loved her brother and was overwrought with emotion every day after he was gone. I recognized a deeper agony in her soul, though, and I knew she wanted and needed to find the peace that Edward had found. One day Freddie and I talked to her, and after reading the same scripture I had read with Edward, we knew her salvation was secure. She became a lovely young lady on both the inside and outside. Jeanette's heart, much like her mother's, was filled with compassion for people.

Frank had already made the commitment to follow Jesus, but Edward's death left him with a stronger desire to live his life to glorify God. Frank worked hard as a salesman for Baker-Lockwood, and he met a lot of famous people. He led many of his business contacts into faith in Jesus. He had always sung at our meetings, but it seemed to me that his beautiful baritone voice had a clearer, sweeter tone than it ever had before.

The effect of Edward's death on the younger boys was not immediately evident to me, so I decided to give them time to process their grief before I pressed them about their salvation. I prayed for them and asked that the Lord would give me wisdom about the time and way to talk with them. George and Paul were still very young, but I felt like Wallace and Bert were old enough to make that decision.

Our lease was coming due on our house, and Freddie wanted to move. She found it too painful to stay in the place where her son had died. We found another house a few blocks away, and moved.

I was thankful for the help we received from the church and from friends. Eva was a great help to our family as always, but she was developing her own friends and often went places with them in the evenings. One day Eva wanted to talk to Freddie and me privately. She had met a young man named Mal Dorton, who was the manager of a club. It concerned us that he might not be a good influence on Eva, but she said he was a good man and she was in love with him. She wanted our blessing to marry him. I told her that we would need to meet him, so we arranged an evening for Mal to come and have dinner at our home.

The day came and the house was filled with wonderful smells. Freddie had cooked a delicious pot roast with potatoes and carrots. She baked an apple pie for dessert. Eva helped with all the preparations, but she was obviously nervous about how the evening would unfold. Would the boys behave and not embarrass her? Would Mal like the taste of the food? Would Mal say or do something to offend the people she loved? Finally, a knock at the door told us the time had come. I thought Mal was probably even more nervous on the other side of that door than Eva was. Eva answered and invited her beau inside.

Freddie and I immediately liked Mal. He was polite but quiet. We learned that Mal had grown up in Edwardsville, a small community west of Kansas City. His father was dead and Mal had

stayed to take care of his mother. Because he worked late into the night most of the time, he slept during the day. He had never been to church.

"He's never been to church," I heard Bert snicker to Wallace. I gave them a stern look and they didn't say another word. Eva smiled at me in relief, then went to the kitchen to serve the apple pie. It tasted delicious, and Mal told her so. We excused the boys and Jeanette, and they went outside to play until the sun set. Freddie and I had so many questions that we hardly knew where to begin.

Eva had met Mal through one of her girlfriends who worked as a waitress at the club. Mal did not own the club, but his duties included ordering supplies and hiring people, making sure everything ran smoothly, and manual work, such as arranging tables. I asked him if he would come by some day before work so we could talk more. I thought it would be best to ask him more personal questions one-on-one.

After a good visit, Mal complimented Freddie and Eva on the meal and left to go check in at work. I helped Freddie clear the table, but couldn't resist watching as Eva walked with him to the sidewalk and stood there for a few minutes to say good-bye. Finally, Mal bent over and gave her a kiss. Freddie scolded me for invading their private moment. I hoped Bert and Wallace weren't watching so Eva wouldn't have to endure their teasing.

A few days later Mal came to the house in the early afternoon before school was out. I greeted him at the door and led him to my study. I offered him a seat, then asked if he'd like some coffee. He nodded, so I asked Eva, who was standing in the hallway, to brew some. She went to the kitchen and I returned to the room. I wanted Mal to feel comfortable, but I knew I must find out more about him. Since I was not Eva's real father and my own children were not married, I did not quite know what my role would be. We talked about the beautiful weather and how we had come to Kansas City from Illinois. Mal had always lived in Edwardsville. I asked him if he ever read the Bible. An awkward silence followed. Eva broke the silence when she brought in a tray with two cups of coffee, cream, and sugar. She recognized that her presence at that moment was adding to Mal's discomfort, and she left us alone again. Mal told me that his father had been mean. He had never allowed Mal to attend school, therefore Mal did not know how to read or write. After his father died, his mother needed him to work and provide for them. He loved Eva (and who wouldn't!) and they planned to live with his mother.

He was able to hide his illiteracy at work by cleverly having his employees read for him, and by memorizing labels and symbols. I knew he would be sleeping on Sunday mornings, so church would be out of the question. Eva could still come, though. We talked about the Lord and he said he believed in Jesus. I left it at that and gave my blessing. We walked out the door and told Eva and Freddie. Eva squealed and the wedding plans began.

We had a fancy wedding for Mal and Eva at our home. I walked Eva down the stairs to meet her groom. The ceremony was beautiful and all our friends came, but shortly after their wedding I felt I had done a terrible thing. Eva still visited us occasionally and came to the gospel meetings alone, but we rarely saw Mal. He was always at work or asleep. The care of Mal's elderly mother fell completely on Eva's shoulders, but she never complained. Time passed, and then we rarely saw Eva, either.

I traveled a lot more after this, regularly going to rural areas along the rail lines in Kansas and Missouri. I would be gone for four or five days and then come home for a few days. When I was home I helped Freddie with the housework, but often I would meet someone on the street or in a meeting and invite him to our house for dinner without thinking about the extra food that would be necessary, much like I'd done in the past. Once again Freddie got used to the possibility of extra guests, and without complaining, she prepared more than we needed for our family. If we didn't have guests, there was always a homebound person from church who welcomed the chance to have one of Freddie's home-cooked meals. Without knowing it, we were being trained and prepared for the next step in our spiritual journey.

For several years we had been hoping to hold the Plymouth Brethren's annual conference in Kansas City. The dates were finally set—September 27–29, 1907. Freddie and I were on the committee to plan the event. In Kansas City, Mrs. H. Charles, John Lockwood, George Trittle and his wife, and of course C. J. and his wife were all

involved. We knew C. J. and I could do much of the speaking, and we also wanted to give Walter Wilson an opportunity. He was becoming a regular speaker in Kansas City and was especially popular with young people. In the Plymouth Brethren tradition all are taught to be able to tell the gospel, so there were plenty of locally available speakers. We also invited Robert Miller from Scotland, Roland Smith from Santa Rosa, California, Andrew Walley from Montrose, Missouri, and Annabelle Kerr from Chicago. Roland Smith had daughters that were friends of Jeanette. We had met them in Chicago, and the girls were looking forward to the time together. We could all see that our daughters were developing lifelong friendships, and both families were very pleased. The three days would be filled with music, messages, fellowship, and food. Tents from C. J.'s shop would be set up and filled with folding chairs.

Letters had to be written, accommodations had to be made for guest speakers, flyers had to be made and distributed, ads had to be placed in newspapers and other publications—these and many other preparations were underway. It took a lot of our time. We bought a small printing press and set it up in our basement. We were able to print tracts, flyers, and brochures in our own home. The younger boys loved to help with the printing and bundling of our material.

Frank prepared several songs to sing. As I have mentioned, his voice was more beautiful than ever after Edward's death, and he was planning to sing several special songs during the conference. I could see Frank's faith growing even though he was often among worldly

people at work. He had made contact with people in the movie industry in California. Cecile B. DeMille often had parties and invited Frank, but I never worried about him. He kept himself free from the temptations that overtook a lot of his acquaintances. Even so, Frank was likable and people enjoyed being around him.

Wallace and Bert ran errands and helped wherever we asked. At each of the evening services, the whole Capp family was clean, on time, and sitting near the front of the tent. We stayed late every night to help with the cleanup and setup for the next day.

The conference was a huge success. People came from the United States as well as from all over the world. We enjoyed seeing old friends from Chicago and making new friends. The gospel was preached and many people were saved.

Frank Capp

Chapter Twenty-One

Santa

One beautiful fall day in 1908 Frank came to me and asked if we could talk. He wanted to tell me about a plan he and five other men had discussed. "What do you think about Santa Claus?" he asked. His question took me by surprise.

We had always enthusiastically celebrated the birth of the Savior in our home, but had not ever mentioned Santa. The joyful songs, the decorations, the wonderful foods…I loved Christmas, but I wasn't sure about Santa. The character was based on St. Nicholas, but I knew very little about him. The concept of sainthood belonged to the Catholic Church in my mind, and the Plymouth Brethren were solidly against superiority among believers. Slowly, the words "I don't know" came out of my mouth.

Frank told me about the men involved. One was a doctor, one was an actor, one was a wealthy businessman, another was a common worker, and the last was a salesman like Frank. They wanted to remain anonymous, but I was glad Frank shared with me their names. I knew they were all men of strong Christian faith. I promised not to reveal their identities. Each one knew children who needed some joy in their lives. Children in hospitals, orphanages, churches, and in private homes were on their lists.

The plan was for all of the men to collect toys, clothes, and food. On Christmas Eve Frank, dressed in a red suit and having the best physique for the role, would deliver the items. The men would drive him in a car and drop him off a block away. Then Frank was to walk to the house, stomp his boots on the porch, jingle some bells and with a loud voice yell "Whoa" followed by a jolly laugh. He would distribute the appropriate toys to each child and slip out when the children became occupied with their new gifts. Then he would run to the end of the block to meet his friends who would have a new supply of gifts in another car. They envisioned this repeating for hours until all the goodies were delivered. "Dad, I just want to give joy," he said. "I can slip a tract to the parents or guardians that tells them about Jesus."

I could tell Frank was already excited about the possibilities, and after all, Jesus loved children. It gave me joy to see Frank's eyes light up when he talked about it. I told him to let me know if I could help. As he bounded out the door he turned and asked, "Do you think

Ma could sew a red suit to fit me?" I knew Freddie would love sewing his costume.

During the next few weeks I saw Freddie and Frank designing the red coat, pants, and hat with white trim, a white wig, and a long beard. Finally, Frank asked her to make him several large red drawstring bags. The costume was taking shape, but no one saw it except Freddie and me.

I began reading about St. Nicholas of Myra. He lived in 300 A.D. and was known for his generosity, just as my son was. Frank was a perfect fit for the role. Still, I wanted to be sure Frank was glorifying Jesus in this venture, not himself or a man who lived a long time ago in Turkey. Frank and I had many more discussions about this.

The preparations for Christmas were beginning at our house, too. I had speaking engagements in various places, and each time I came home Freddie was doing a new Christmas project with the younger children from church, sewing another holiday dress, or practicing Christmas songs.

The warm dry air had lingered longer than usual that year and it seemed like all the preparations were untimely and artificial. But a week before Christmas we finally got some snow. Four inches. The children were excited and it seemed like Christmas was truly here.

On Christmas Eve, donned in his new suit, Frank left the house to meet his companions. He was hoping no one would see him

prematurely. Everyone arrived on time. They had practiced the route and knew exactly how long each transition would take. They couldn't be sure how long each visit would last, but they had four cars filled and in position. As each car was emptied, the driver would then go home to be with his own family. Frank stayed in character. Later he told me that with each delivery, his heart had swelled with joy from the smiles, kisses, and hugs of happy boys and girls as well as tears of gratitude from parents. The transitions were fun. The men laughed heartily when they saw Frank exit the house and run down the street. Their fast-paced switching of bags was comical. Sometimes Frank would hear barking and prayed the dog or dogs were behind a fence. If they could, Frank's friends distracted the uncontained dogs so Frank didn't have to worry about them.

After the final delivery, Frank's last friend gave him a ride home. "Santa" was exhausted, but he knew they would do it again. At our house, Paul, who was eleven years old, was the youngest. The whole family agreed to keep Frank's secret, but we also enjoyed seeing him as Santa, knowing he transformed back to our dear Frank when the red suit came off.

After Christmas I studied and prepared for a trip to Chicago. I was scheduled to preach nightly in March for an entire week. I would see some of our old friends while I was there. Freddie wanted to go too, but she didn't want to leave home. Jeanette, now seventeen, had just started a new job as a clerk at McKeen Dry Goods and was also going to night school. Wallace was restless and wanted to leave. His

immaturity disturbed both Freddie and me. I remembered how determined I had been to leave home and I could see that same attitude in Wallace. By summer he had boarded a westbound train for Denver.

For the next few years our lives were fairly simple. Freddie worked at home and at Central Bible Hall, and I traveled to speak at small towns across Kansas and Missouri. I was beginning to feel the weariness of so much travel. I was tired, but preaching the gospel always energized me again, even though I looked forward to coming home to Freddie's good cooking and my own comfortable bed after every trip.

Frank, Wallace, Bert, and George all worked at Baker-Lockwood in different capacities during those years. Jeanette became skilled at business and was a valuable employee wherever she worked. Wallace wrote to his mother and sister occasionally, but he didn't seem to have a job or any idea what he was going to do. He had tried to join the Army in Kansas City, but was refused due to flat feet. He said a guy had told him that the Army was recruiting in Wyoming, so he might try going there. Meanwhile, a girl Wallace's age from Central Bible Hall had family in Denver. Her name was Nell Kendrick and she was studying to be a nurse. Her uncle owned a copper mining company and Wallace thought Mr. Kendrick might hire him. It was obvious that Wallace loved the mountains. On one postcard there was a picture of him dressed as a miner and the words "On the road to ruin." I hoped they were not words of prophecy for my son.

Changes were coming soon. I saw how my absence had—and still was—deeply affecting my relationships with my children, but I didn't know how to change that.

Chapter Twenty-Two

Alpena Pass

Our lives were full and busy. The children were becoming adults. I knew they would someday make their own choices, so it didn't surprise me when Bert decided to leave Baker–Lockwood and take a job with Levi Strauss denim company. In October of 1913 he and Ada Rose Stundick got married. Bert was the first of our children to leave home and we knew the others would soon follow. Wallace was still the one I was most concerned about. He never seemed at peace. I tried to talk to him about salvation, but he was not interested. Edward's death did not leave him tender to God as it had the other children. Instead, it hardened his heart. He came back home from his trip to Colorado in late 1912. He was unable to find steady work out there and his plans to join the Army did not work out there either because of his flat feet. He took a job as a cashier with the Union Pacific railroad and at night he went to school to learn accounting.

Even so, he just seemed so lost. I wanted him to come with me, but he wouldn't hear of it.

Freddie and I were active at the Gospel Hall as well as at home, but the Lord was calling me to go into new and different places to hold tent meetings. Like the apostle Paul, I kept in contact with those congregations where I had seen the Holy Spirit use my words to bring people to salvation in Jesus Christ. I felt a responsibility, as I did with my children, to help those new disciples grow in their faith. I often went to Belleville, Kansas, to assist in the work being done there and to Bloomfield, Arkansas, where I had often held meetings.

Now God seemed to have a new plan for me. On my visits to Bloomfield, I had heard of the people they called hillbillies in the Ozark Mountains to the southeast of Bloomfield. The people were poor and lived in small shacks deep in the hills. They had little food or clothes and even less hope. Moonshine and violence were common and they rarely had contact with civilization. I knew that God was calling me to tell them about the Savior, so I went to C. J. Baker for counsel and prayers about a trip there.

I told Freddie that I needed to spend a longer time in Arkansas and that I didn't know how long. She knew that it would be difficult or impossible for me to send her word from that area since she had not received the telegram about Edward while she was at her brother's house in southern Missouri. We prayed with C. J. and looked at maps of the railroad line through northern Arkansas. I would go east from

Rogers toward Harrison and get off the train somewhere along the pass. We decided I would go after the snow melted in the spring.

As was our custom, two men from Central Bible Hall accompanied me. For this trip we chose my son Bert and William Sommerville. Bert and Ada were expecting our first grandchild in June so we planned on coming back before the birth.

It was a crisp clear day in late April 1915 and I kissed Freddie good-bye in Kansas City. We loaded my canvas "Two Roads" chart, several songbooks, and a box of tracts. We didn't know how useful the tracts would be since we didn't know if the people were able to read or not. As the train rolled out of the station, I prayed and put my life and this work totally in God's hands.

The trip from Kansas City to Bloomfield was familiar to me. At Bloomfield we stepped out of the train and stretched our legs. The air was cool but the sun shone down, warming us pleasantly. We unloaded all our baggage, including the tent, and stacked it in a pile on the wooden platform. It would be a couple of hours before the Northern Arkansas train would be ready to board, so we sat on a bench and ate the lunch we had packed.

When we finished we took a walk and found a shop where ancient artifacts from the area were sold. Bloomfield was named after Clarence Bloomfield Moore, an archeologist from Philadelphia who had done extensive exploration in the area. I saw a small collection of Indian arrowheads in the shop that were very unique. I thought that

since Wallace enjoyed the Wild West, he might be interested in them. I mentioned it to Bert and he agreed. I talked to the shop owner and asked how much they cost. It seemed like a lot of money for them, so I offered him less. He made sure to point out that it took Mr. Moore over forty years to collect these spearheads along the White River, and they were extremely rare. After some bargaining we finally reached a price and I bought them, even convincing him to include a small wooden box lined with cotton fibers for storing them.

When the train arrived we showed our tickets to the conductor and began loading everything again. After a few minutes we were settled into our seats. All of us wanted to sit by a window so we could take in the new scenery. The train headed south toward Eureka Springs, then toward Harrison. The landscape was beautiful. Soon I realized the hills had become bigger and the valleys deeper. The waterfalls and rocky bluffs reminded me of the mountains in Pennsylvania, yet they were different. White, pink, and red blooms occasionally popped through the drapery of green. According to our conductor, the blooms were on dogwood and redbud trees. God's beauty was on display everywhere we looked.

The train passed through small communities and sometimes stopped to deliver freight. There were hardly any passengers boarding and even fewer leaving the train. As the train came to a halt at the small wooden platforms, we saw groups of people staring at us. Their faces showed lines of hardness. The children scurried around, barefooted and curious. The adults seemed guarded and suspicious of

us. We watched them from the train windows, taking in all we could. I wondered what they thought of us, but I was sure these people needed the hope that only the gospel brings. I prayed and asked God to show us when and how to speak to them. We were invading their territory, and only the Holy Spirit could prepare their hearts and at the same time equip us with wisdom for this endeavor.

Our tickets would take us to Harrison, but as we went through towns like Cave Springs, Little Flock, Eureka Springs, Berryville, and Green Forest, I saw the same despair at each stop. Finally, at Alpena Pass, I jumped out of my seat and said to Bert and William, "We're getting off here." They looked at me like I had caught on fire. Maybe I had. We walked toward the door and began to retrieve our luggage.

The conductor said, "This is not your stop."

I told him, "Yes, it is. This is exactly where God wants us to be." After a couple of minutes of confusion, we convinced him that we were getting off at this stop. Bert and William had seen me choose what seemed like illogical places to take the gospel, so they didn't question my decision. As the train departed, Bert, William, and I, along with our luggage, tent, and boxes of songbooks and tracts, were sitting on the wooden platform of Alpena Pass, Arkansas.

It was like stepping into another world, one in which we were not sure we were welcome. A couple of men with long beards sat on a log a few feet away smoking corncob pipes and whittling on sticks

with small knives. They glanced at me and then went back to their work. I prayed and asked the Lord again to protect and guide us.

Across a dirt road we saw a wooden building that looked a little like a boarding house. On the side was written "Mollie and Ducks" in bright red letters. We left our things on the platform and walked to the building. Inside the door were two girls. It was hard to tell how old they were, but they seemed to belong there. One of them said, "Need a place to stay?" I was shocked to think this girl was offering three strange men a room. I couldn't imagine Nettie in such a place.

The girl told us that her name was Mary, but everyone called her Mollie. "This is my sister, Margaret, but we call her Duck," she said. "You can have a room and vittles for two dollars per night. Are ye staying long?"

I was still trying to get over my shock when I said, "Not sure."

"Well, just let us know. We don't have many visitors, but we need to know how much vittles to fix."

I wondered what vittles were, but I said, "Fine. We'll get our things from the train station." Bert and William looked at the girls and then me, unbelieving, but they started walking back to our pile of belongings. I took out two dollars from my pocket and paid her.

Mollie showed us the room. It was small and didn't have a key. We put our things inside and looked at the two small beds. One of us

would have to sleep on the floor, but it was a roof over our heads. "Duck will come and get ye for supper." It was getting late and the sun would be setting soon, so we moved the tent to the side of the building for the night. Tomorrow we would figure out where to set it up.

Duck came and led us to the dining area where Mollie introduced us to her father. She'd told us her mother had died a year earlier, and that's when the girls had come up with the idea of starting a hotel. With the new railroad, they thought a hotel would be needed. Their father was silent. Duck whispered to me, "Pa ain't been right since Ma died. He don't work. Just too sad." I nodded.

I learned that the vittles they'd talked about was food. They served some kind of meat. Bert and William later told me they thought it was squirrel. Then there were mushrooms, biscuits, and gravy. We ate and tried not to ask too many questions.

"Folks are gonna want to know why youse are here," Mollie said.

"Well," I answered, "We have a tent."

"What?" she asked. "Then why'd you need our room?"

"Oh, the tent isn't for sleeping in. It's for our meetings."

"What meetin's?" she asked. I could tell she was questioning her judgment in character and was suspicious about our intentions.

"Well, we go to towns and have tent meetings to tell people the good news."

"What good news? You ain't gonna bring another railroad through here, are ye?"

"Oh no. We tell about the good news of Jesus."

"Well I don't know about that, but folks here ain't too keen on strangers bringin' in new ideas." The conversation seemed to come to an end, and she cleared the table and took the dishes to a tub of water to wash them in. There was no indoor plumbing, and I didn't see where Duck got the bucket of water. Mollie quipped over her shoulder, "Best hit the hay."

"Good night," I said.

"Night," she answered.

In our room, William decided to be the first to take the floor. He took a blanket off one of the beds and stretched it out on the wood floor. We all lay down and talked until our minds could no longer process the things we had seen and heard. We knew that the morning would bring new challenges.

***

All too soon the sunlight and the sound of a rooster crowing greeted us. It was morning. We got up and looked for a place to wash

up. Finding none, we decided to explore the area. We didn't see any sign of Mollie or Duck. I wondered if it had all been a dream. We found a small stream behind the hotel and went there to wash up. The water was cold, and yet it felt good. As we walked back to the hotel, Mollie approached us and offered us some bread, cheese, and milk. We ate all of it. She asked what we were fixin' to do today. We told her we needed to find a place to pitch the tent and that we would need some help. She told us about the store where you could usually find some of the local men "jawin'." There was another one of those words I didn't exactly understand, but so far Mollie had been a great help to us.

We walked down the road a little way and found another wooden building. We had not noticed it the night before. In the same red paint as the hotel were the words, "Whitaker's Cash Store and Meat Market." We went inside and saw a group of men.

"Need somthin'?" one of them asked.

"Not particularly." I scanned the contents of the store. It looked like almost anything you could think of was available there even if it was used and rusty. I knew I would be back to this place to supply us with any tools or hardware we might need during our stay. After a few minutes of browsing I asked, "Is there a good place to set up a tent around here?"

"A tent?" the man who seemed to be the owner asked.

"Maybe down by the tracks." Another man snickered, followed by laughter from the group.

Realizing that we were the brunt of their amusement, I calmly responded by saying, "Thank you." I told Bert and William to take the tent down by the tracks and start setting it up.

"Wait. Are ye really goin' to set up a tent?" the owner asked.

"Sure," I said. "Want to help? We need to get it up for the meeting tonight." I could see that all this talk about tents and meetings was starting to get attention.

"Nobody told us 'bout no meetin'," the loud man shouted.

"What's it for?" another spit out.

"We really do need some help. Come and help and we'll tell you more," I said. I walked toward the door. "Bring your hammers," I added as the spring door slammed behind me.

A group of men grabbed hammers and followed me out of the store. Bert and William were already dragging the huge bundle that was the tent from the hotel. A few of the men saw them, ran over, and gave them a hand. We unwrapped the canvas and started assembling the poles. As we worked together I got to know the men a little better. Fred and Edwin Whitaker were brothers who owned the store. Hezzie Summers was a simple farmer, about fifty years old. Finis Porter was younger, but also a farmer, and he had a bunch of kids. Hugh Plumlee

was the loud farmer, and Arch Brown was the mail carrier. I wondered how these men had time to put all other work aside and help us. It seemed to me that there was no urgency about any work here, but their curiosity cancelled their daily routines. When we brought out the "Two Roads" canvas, the men stared at it like a puzzle. I told them I would explain it at the meeting, hoping to give them incentive to come. Duck and Mollie saw the poles and canvas taking on shape and brought a bucket of water with a ladle for us to drink from. The cold water was refreshing

By the time the sun was high in the sky, the tent was in place next to the train tracks, just beyond the wooden platform and station where we had unloaded it. Now we needed places to sit. The men brought some extra railroad ties and set them up as benches. We thanked the men and told them to bring their families to the meeting at six o'clock.

We went back to the hotel carrying the empty water bucket, and Mollie had some more vittles ready. Again, we weren't quite sure what the food was, but we ate graciously. Duck told us the greens were dandelion plants. Mollie said she was makin' a special treat for supper—gooseberry pie. I wasn't sure I would ever get used to these unusual meals.

We went back to our room and I started preparing my message for the evening meeting. I wondered if these people even knew what a Jew was and if my story would mean anything to them. I wondered if any of them had ever seen a Bible or would know anything about

Jesus. I knew I had to use the "Two Roads" canvas, but maybe the story about Edward's death would be better to start with. I prayed again for guidance.

After a while I said, "Let's go fishing." Bert and William knew I wasn't talking about actually fishing for fish. We would "cast our net" and see who we would catch. So we went on a walk.

We started down the road beyond the Whitaker's store. We didn't see anyone outside. It wasn't long before the road became a path in the woods. There was no denying that this place was beautiful in a primitive way. We heard some voices and walked through the woods toward them. About a quarter mile down the path we found a clearing. Two men were working in a field. When they saw us, they quit talking and stared. Then the older one ran to a small cabin. He came out with a shotgun and yelled for us to go away. I told him we meant no harm, but he still held the gun on us. I told him our names and that we just wanted to talk. I saw two women through the window of the cabin. The man continued to point the gun toward us and warned us to leave. So we turned around and went back down the path toward Whitaker's. It was obvious that not all the people at Alpena were friendly, and this assignment wasn't necessarily going to be as easy as I had hoped.

Chapter Twenty-Three

Success in Arkansas

The meetings were going well. I was surprised how easy the words came to me. God showed me how to mix my personal stories about my childhood, Edward's death, and my candy business with the gospel. For a week, people came and listened. Each evening God brought people from every corner of the countryside. Some of the faces became familiar to me as they returned night after night, and sometimes they brought new faces.

The first night, after I had finished with my message, I gave an invitation to receive the free gift of salvation. There was a long, silent pause. William, Bert, and I looked around the tent to see any hint of response. I wondered if they had understood. It was awkward, and I didn't know what to do next. Finally, Hezzie Summers stood up and walked forward. Next, Lee Grisham, Finis Porter and his family, Hugh

Plumlee, and many others stepped up. It was all we could do to lead each of them in a prayer of salvation and speak a little more with each one. Our hearts were thrilled, and we knew the Lord was pleased as well. The second night even more people came forward. There were old people and young people, men and women, farmers and businessmen. Everyone seemed to be ready to hear and receive the Good News. By the third night a regular group kept coming back to hear more, but new faces still appeared. I knew, as each night progressed, that the Lord was at work and hearts were being changed.

One night Dr. Watkins, the local doctor, came in his two-horse buggy. He listened as I told Bible stories of Jesus and the apostles' ability to heal. He was fascinated, and I knew that message was custom tailored by the Holy Spirit for him. After the service he and I talked for quite some time about the spiritual aspect of healing. Then he put his trust in Jesus and received salvation. I told him about Walter Wilson in Kansas City, and I knew that if Walter and Dr. Watkins would meet, there would be some lively medical and spiritual discussions.

During the day we would go visit homes and build friendships. We found the hill people to be very friendly once they got to know us. We often ate meals with different families. The strange food started to taste good to us and we never refused anything they offered. Like Peter, we didn't want to consider anything "unclean" that God had provided for us.

After a week, Bert wanted to get back home to Ada since the baby would be born soon. We said good-bye to Bert, then William and I continued to hold meetings. The "Two Roads" canvas took time to explain, and yet the people patiently studied with us. They were excited to hear and understand God's plan for the end times.

The man who had pointed the gun at us and threatened us that first day showed up at the tent one night, shotgun in his hand. He still had that scowl on his face, and I was afraid of what he might do. His family was with him, and they sat on the log at the back of the tent. Some of those who came regularly stared at the family on that log and even pulled away from them. I began to preach.

When I offered the invitation, the man put his shotgun down on the ground and walked toward me. I prayed silently that God had truly touched this man's heart and that he wouldn't harm me or anyone else who was present. With a gravelly voice he said, "Does this Jesus really love mean people like me?"

"Yes," I replied.

"Why?"

"Because He created all of us to have a relationship with God, and that means everyone. Even mean ones."

"What do I have to do?"

"Believe that God sent His son Jesus and that He died for your sins and He rose again from the grave."

"Well, I do," the man said, and his face reflected sincerity.

"Welcome to God's family, then. By the way, what's your name?"

"Jim Ward, and I beg your pardon that I scared you with my gun."

Then and there a "mean one" was added to the Kingdom of God. I ate dinner with Jim's family the next day and all of them came to faith.

I wrote daily letters to Freddie telling her about our work in Alpena, and she wrote back to me. Every time I saw Arch Brown, he would either pick up my letters or deliver one from Freddie. According to Freddie, the children were doing fine. Frank was at the State Fair in Kansas as he had done almost every summer. Jeanette was spending time with friends after work, and one boy was particularly interested in courting her. I knew I would need to meet this young man when I returned home. Wallace was difficult, of course, and he wanted to go back to Chicago. Freddie said she might go with him. The other boys were working hard. Ada's time to have the baby was very near, and she was glad Bert had come home.

The news about Wallace disturbed me, and I decided it was time to write to him and send the arrowheads for his birthday. I prayed

that God would guide him. I thought perhaps Wallace should come and take Bert's place here. Maybe that would help him learn to appreciate his good life. I had to admit that I was feeling angry and disappointed in him. I sealed the envelope, put a stamp on it, and went to find Arch. I knew he could help me package the box of arrowheads so that it would arrive undamaged.

I didn't know if it was the heat, the stress, or the unusual food I was eating, but I began to feel weak and dizzy. I needed naps several times a day. I tried to reserve my energy so that I could preach in the evening. William was worried that something serious might be wrong with me. He talked to Dr. Watkins and the good doctor visited me. My symptoms didn't indicate a clear diagnosis, though. Rest and staying out of the sun seemed like the only treatment for now, but I spent large portions of time in the Word as well.

Sometimes people would come to me to ask questions, and I needed to be available as much as possible. Some days I would feel fine and other days I would be weak. Mollie and Duck checked on me and brought me anything I needed.

As the summer lingered on, I knew it was time to go back home. The congregation here had a strong foundation. A Bible church was being formed and I would return to check on them. It appeared that every single one who had come to our meetings was now saved.

I bought a ticket home for William and me, and some of the same men who set up the tent helped take it down. The conversations

as we worked were much different now than they had been a few months earlier. Then, they were skeptical and curious. Now, they were born again and shared the scriptures that they had read that morning. We prayed together and sang a few more songs. Leaving was bittersweet for me, but I knew God was leading me somewhere else now.

As William and I boarded the train, we were excited to get back home, yet we felt like we were leaving another home. We waved out the window and a crowd of faces smiled and waved back. We knew these faces now.

The conductor on the train had heard about our meetings in Alpena and asked us lots of questions. He, too, gave his life to Jesus. He asked us if we had ever been to Oklahoma. We had not.

"Well, there's some folks who have recently settled over there who probably need to hear about God. There's a train line to Muskogee and Henryetta. Soon the railroad will go all the way out to New Mexico, too." We told him we would pray about that.

I slept most of the way back to Kansas City. We had so much to share and were anxious to see our families again.

Chapter Twenty-Four

Jeanette's Beau

I stepped off the train in Kansas City and there to meet me were Freddie, Jeanette, Bert, George, and Paul. Frank was traveling for Baker–Lockwood, and Wallace—well, who knew where Wallace was. The shock on my family's faces told me that something about my appearance had changed in the weeks I had been gone. Freddie came to me and gently took my face in her hands. "You're so thin!" she exclaimed. "Do you feel well?"

I had not thought my health had failed so much as to be noticeable. I was tired, but I had not looked in a mirror for a long time. William reunited with his family, then went over to Bert, George, and Paul, and they talked quietly. Finally, William said to me that he wanted to go home, but he would talk to me in a day or two. My family was whizzing me off to the car to take me to our house.

Jeanette and Freddie had a big dinner prepared and friends would be coming to eat with us. Among them would be C. J. Baker and Walter Wilson, and I was anxious to speak with both of them.

The moment I walked into the house, the sweet aromas of Freddie's cooking filled my lungs. It had been so long since I'd tasted the wonderful foods of home. We prayed and sat down to the table. Wallace showed up almost unnoticed, except by me. His eyes and mine connected but he quickly found his seat and joined one of the many conversations around the table.

After dinner, C. J., Walter, and I went out on the front porch to talk. I told Walter about Dr. Watkins and how I believed they would enjoy each other's company. Walter asked me about my health. I told him I'd been tired, but I didn't think it was serious, and Dr. Watkins couldn't determine what it could be other than heat exhaustion. Walter told me about a new disease he had been reading about called diabetes. He suggested that I come by his office so he could test me. I agreed to do that soon.

C. J. and I talked about the possibilities of my next trip. Perhaps I should go to Oklahoma and then maybe New Mexico. We agreed it would be best to wait for a few months, but we would pray about it and do some research. He was thrilled to hear about the work at Alpena Pass. He said Bert came back proclaiming that every person at the meetings had been saved. I confirmed that this was a fairly accurate account.

I went back inside and took some time to meet my first grandchild, Maurice Capp. Bert had returned just a few days before his birth, and now the parents and baby were a happy family. I had always loved babies, and this was a new generation of Capp children for me to love. I could tell Freddie loved her new role as Grandma. Maurice was a happy, joyful child.

Then there was Wallace. I loved that boy, but he made it so difficult for us. Now, he wanted to go to Colorado again. I wondered if he would ever settle down. He didn't want to talk to me, but I asked him if he had received the arrowheads.

"Yes," he said. "Can I go now?" I didn't know what to say, so I just nodded my head and let him walk out the door.

Jeanette had cleared the table, washed the dishes, and waited patiently for me to come to her. She was so excited to tell me about her boyfriend, but she wanted to have my full attention first. She had grown into a beautiful woman, and her sweet personality would make her a prize for any young man. "Oh Daddy, I am in love," she said. I smiled and listened as she told me all about the boy who worked with her at Allen and Bayne. He was Mr. Allen's son, Harvey.

"He sounds like a great fellow, Nettie. When can I meet him?" She said she would bring him home after work one day soon. I kissed her on the cheek and then told her I really needed some sleep. The trip had been long and my body was ready for rest again.

She said, "I understand, Daddy. I love you."

Freddie saw our guests out and then finished the cleaning before she joined me in our bed. It was so good to be home, but I was asleep before she had the chance to say a word. She knew there would be time the next day for us to talk, but I was sad I hadn't saved any time and energy for her. The weeks I had been gone were probably most difficult for her.

***

The next morning I awoke to the clatter of dishes in the kitchen. Freddie was already hard at work making breakfast for the boys and Jeanette. I heard their muffled voices as they got ready and then were out the door to their jobs. I felt a sense of accomplishment that my children were productive adults. Even Wallace, though so distant, was working as an accountant for the railroad. I wondered how late he had stayed out the night before.

Freddie was quietly reading her Bible in the living room when I finally got dressed and came out of the bedroom. She asked me if I had slept well, and I told her I had. Concern creased her brow, but she didn't ask any more about my health. I knew she wanted all the details, though.

"I'm fine," I told her. "Dinner was wonderful last night." Then she hugged me, and I was so weak I thought I would fall and take her with me. I found my way to the chair and sat down.

"What do you think of Nettie's beau?" I asked, trying to change the subject. Freddie only commented that he seemed like a very nice boy. "Is he saved?"

"I don't know. He wants to meet you, though." That was a good sign, I thought. This was a new experience for me. Although I had given away Eva, this was different. Nettie was young and I didn't want to make any mistakes. Eva and her husband Mal were still married, but his life as a nightclub manager made it very difficult. They never went to church.

The rest of the day, Freddie and I caught up with each other. She told me about her trip to Chicago and of our friends that she was able to visit. Wallace went out with his friends, and she saw little of him while they were there. I was sure that she was just as concerned about him as I was. He had bought a motorcycle with some of his money and could go anywhere he wanted on it.

I did a few chores around the house, and it felt good to work with my hands a little. We had an old printing machine in our basement, and in my spare time I printed tracts that we could use at Central Bible Hall or at the tent meetings. I had left all the tracts we took to Arkansas at Alpena for the fledgling church to give to visitors.

Freddie began making dinner, and the boys came home from work. Around five thirty Jeanette came home with her guest. "Daddy, I'd like for you to meet Harvey Allen," she said. The young man put out his hand for me to shake and I took it.

"Glad to meet you, Harvey" We all gathered around the table for a delicious meal. Harvey was polite and gracious. We prayed as always, and I saw Harvey moving his hand, touching his forehead, chest, and then each shoulder. I knew that was the sign Catholics use at the end of their prayers, and my heart sank. Did Nettie know he was a Catholic? Surely she knew my feelings about Catholicism. How could this be? I could not—no, I *would* not, let her marry a Catholic. Even so, I remained silent through the rest of the meal.

After dinner I asked Nettie to excuse Harvey and me so that we could talk. She smiled and seemed more than ready to let us have our discussion. I was sure she thought it was going to end with a proposal and with everyone happy, but I knew that was unlikely.

In my study, Harvey told me he loved Nettie and would like to court her and then marry her. My face must have betrayed me. His smiling face suddenly turned serious. "What's wrong?" he asked.

"Young man," I said, "you seem like a very nice guy, but I would like to know this. Are you Catholic?"

"Why, yes I am," he responded. "I love God with all my heart and I love your daughter."

"Do you know that means your church would not accept her?" I asked.

"She can convert," he said, and I almost exploded.

"No, she can't."

"But sir, we love each other," he answered.

"No, No, No." I yelled this time. I was sure Nettie could hear me from the hallway.

"I think I should go," Harvey said, and he left the room. He hugged Nettie on the way out, told her that they would talk later, and left her alone in the hallway with tears welling up in her eyes.

She slowly came into the room and looked at me with a hatred I had never before seen in her eyes, which were now wet with tears. "Daddy! What have you done?"

"Nettie, I love you and only want what's best for you."

"What's best for me is Harvey."

I tried to explain to her that neither his church nor hers would ever accept their marriage, and I was just trying to protect her from being hurt, but she wasn't listening.

"We will elope," she said, defiance in her eyes.

"No you won't. I forbid you to marry him!"

Her tears came full force then, and she ran out of the room, screaming, "I hate you!"

Freddie tried to intervene and comfort her daughter, but it was no use. She was gone, and Freddie and I were reduced to our own puddle of tears.

***

What had I done? I loved Nettie, but I had destroyed her with a few moments of pride and anger. Would I ever see her again? Would she ever forgive me? My heart was crushed, and yet I knew the damage to hers was even worse. If she and Harvey did elope, we would probably never see her again. How did his family respond to their relationship? I wondered, but I never found out. Nettie spent a few days with friends, and when she came home, Harvey's name was never mentioned again. Nettie quit her job at Allen and Bayne and found a job at a bank.

God continued to work on my heart. I remembered the Catholic priest who came to our street meetings in the early days of ministry in Kansas City. I knew God loved Catholics, but their rituals were hard for me to reconcile in my mind. Nettie always respected me after that, but we were never close again. God had given her that sweet, loving personality and she learned, maybe even more than I had, a difficult lesson in forgiveness that day.

Jeannette (Nettie) Capp

Chapter Twenty-Five

Back Home

Several weeks passed before I felt more like myself. The weeks in the Ozarks and the conflict with Nettie had taken its toll on both my body and mind. Meetings with Walter confirmed that I had all the symptoms of diabetes. He kept me informed on the newest studies and treatments. Because I was feeling better, I had trouble focusing on life changes that might benefit me in the future. The main thing I needed to do was adjust my diet to foods low in sugar, but a new way to control blood sugar involved daily insulin injections. He said he would continue to read up on the most current test results. Walter was seriously concerned about my health, even though I was more interested in the next phase of my ministry and where God would take me with the gospel message.

Freddie was glad to have me home and wanted me to spend time with the family. Frank was gone most of the time with his job at Baker–Lockwood and was preaching and singing at the Kansas State Fair as he had done for many years. Bert and Ada were happy new parents. I loved playing with little Maurice, and I finally understood the joy that Christian felt when he was with our boys. Nettie, of course, avoided spending much time with me. She was a successful businesswoman and a leader in several groups that ministered to others. She and her girlfriends traveled often. George and Paul were hard workers and helped Freddie with chores at home. Wallace, still restless, had no interest in talking with me. He and Nettie were close, and I wondered if he, too, was angry with me for spoiling her happiness. Nettie introduced him to several of her girlfriends, and I felt like they were a good influence on him.

I spent my days studying the Bible, writing letters, and visiting people from Central Bible Hall. It was great to reconnect with C. J. and others who had graciously supported my tent meetings. They were anxious to hear the stories about the people I'd met and the experiences I'd had. I had time to check with the congregation in Belleville, Kansas, answer new requests for speaking engagements, and devote large periods of time to prayer.

All the boys were registering for the draft. Not being a man concerned with politics or war, I was not equipped to advise them about those things. I remembered that in Chicago the World's Fair was shortened by an assassination, but it only affected me because our

business had to close sooner than we expected. I knew Kansas City had corruption in politics, but I tried to keep out of any discussions regarding that. And yet, I spoke about being a Jewish anarchist. Although a rebel at heart, I never had a desire to protest against the government of the United States. I followed the laws and registered as an alien every year as required.

One day Walter Wilson asked me an interesting question. "Why haven't you filed to become a United States citizen?" His question took me off guard, but I didn't feel like he was judging me. He was just curious. I didn't know how to answer.

"I don't know," was all I could say. His question spurred a new pursuit for me. How exactly do you become a citizen?

More important to me was the challenge I had been given to preach in Oklahoma. Throughout the winter months, I made plans for a trip in the coming summer. Some of the men in Alpena were excited to help in the outreach across the state line into the newly settled state. I talked with C. J. and the people at Central Bible Hall about this new venture. They easily caught the vision and passion for the lost in Indian Territory. Oklahoma had been a state for almost ten years, but it still seemed wild and untamed. Those who came during the land rush days were settling into homes, farming, and working in the coalmines. It reminded me of the stories Christian Bludorn told me about settling on their land in Dakota Territory in the 1870s. I was excited about the trip, but knew it would take me away from home again for weeks.

Freddie and I had to be in agreement for this to be successful, but most of all I needed to be sure it was God's will and not mine.

The holidays at home were delightful for me, as always. The house buzzed with activity even though the children were adults now. Frank organized his trip as Santa and collected the gifts for children. Many of them had fatherless homes this year due to the war in Europe. Nettie and her friends wrote letters and put together packages for servicemen. Whether I liked it or not, the war touched our lives even here in our safe homes.

Services at Central Bible Hall were so fulfilling. Frank's beautiful voice and the words proclaiming the newborn King refueled me. I was ready to share the story with anyone who would listen.

Freddie and I regularly invited strangers from the streets into our home. Most were grateful for a hot meal and a warm place to stay. During these times I learned a new technique for introducing people to the Savior. We would set up a circle of chairs after the meal, one for each person, and one extra. We explained that the empty chair was for Jesus. He was with us always, and we could introduce our guests to Him. Then we would open the scriptures and share about Jesus, our Savior. We would share about our lives and answer their questions. Then we would invite the guests to receive Jesus' free gift of salvation.

In the spring I learned about a night class held at the Kansas City, Kansas high school that prepares people for naturalization as American citizens. I had no idea at that time how much work would be

involved, but I had an uneasy feeling every time I thought about my situation. I had lived in the United States for over forty years, but had never declared my loyalty to it. I felt like I was reaping the benefits of this wonderful country without making a commitment to it. Surely God wouldn't want me to be a person who takes without giving. Now my children were choosing to serve in the military, and I thought that my proper response would be to support the country they were willing to die for. I signed up for the class, but knew my trip to Oklahoma would limit my participation. I had, however, taken the first step. My teacher was Professor I.B. Morgan. He warned me that this would not be easy, but it would be well worth it.

The plans for our trip to Oklahoma took shape. Rather than a tent, we planned to use Nixon schoolhouse. Although used as a school, it also served as the location for any public meetings in the area. We decided that I would leave in early June and go to Henryetta, Oklahoma, by train. My health continued to improve, and my classes with Professor Morgan occupied much of my time.

I would travel from Kansas City alone, but Lee Grisham from Alpena planned to meet me there to help. We printed new tracts in the basement of my house. Freddie helped to get my clothes, books, and notes in order. Then she prayed with me and for me. We tried to prepare ourselves in every way for this adventure into the wild, unknown territory we had only heard about.

The children knew that although their mother was used to my absence, she might need their help a little more. I knew I could count

on Frank, George, Paul, and of course, Nettie. Wallace spent a lot of time on his motorcycle and was rarely around, especially if work was involved.

Finally, the warm summer day came and I found myself at Union Station again, saying good-bye. I promised to write, and I saw a tear in Freddie's eye. We hugged and kissed, and I boarded the southbound train. We had been married almost thirty-four years, and yet these times never got easier. I was so thankful God had given me such a wonderful wife.

Chapter Twenty-Six

Oklahoma

The train slowed and the conductor announced "Muskogee." It had been a long day, and we were near our destination. Throughout the day on the train, I had read through my notes and prepared an outline for my meetings. As in Alpena, I wasn't sure what to expect. Would there be coal miners, farmers, businessmen, or Indians? Whoever came, I knew the Lord was preparing them, too. The gospel was for all. Everyone was in need of the Savior, and God had chosen me to proclaim it.

My conflict with Nettie and my relationship with Wallace were proof that I was not a perfect father, but I prayed for forgiveness. I prayed for my children and asked for God to restore them to me when I came back this time. I trusted that even though I had made mistakes at home, He would still be able to use me when I spoke. Surely He had

not brought me this far just to pull me from the mission. My salvation story was just as powerful as it had been in Chicago, and I still shed tears when I talked about Edward. The memory of Germany and of my family there was fading, but they were a vital part of my story about disobedience, repentance, salvation, and restoration. I knew people related to rebellion and needed a message of hope. The Bible was my toolbox, and I was ready to take on this new territory for His glory.

The next stop was Henryetta. I got off the train with my luggage and looked around. I didn't see any people on the streets. I walked toward a group of buildings and found the schoolhouse. Apparently, school was out for the summer. It was a white stone, two-story building. The first floor was one large room where our meetings would take place. The second floor held smaller classrooms. That's where I would put my cot and sleep. Soon, a man met me and introduced himself as the school's administrator. He told me to make myself at home, and said he would be available if I had any questions.

I set up the canvas "Two Roads" chart across the chalkboard and then went upstairs to set up my cot. Freddie had packed some sandwiches and apples in my bag, so I sat down on the cot, prayed, and then ate.

I had plans for a week of meetings, but beyond that I wasn't sure what the Lord would do. Lee Grisham was coming from Alpena the next day. He could help spread the word about our meetings and also help with outreach. I looked forward to working with him.

A loud whistle sounded and then the streets were swollen with people. I learned that this was the routine at shift change at the coalmines. The men that were leaving the mine were dirty, sweaty, and obviously tired. Those going into the mine were energized and ready to work. Neither group seemed willing to stop and talk to me, a stranger. So I just watched them as they traded places. In a few minutes the streets were empty again. I went back to my room to read and prepare for the coming days. I was tired, and the air was already very warm. Sleep came early.

***

The next morning the loud blast of the coalmine whistle woke me. It was time for the workers to change places again. I washed up a bit and changed clothes. I looked out the window to the street below. A short distance down the street, I saw what looked like a small café. It didn't take long before my stomach reminded me that I needed to eat again, so I walked downstairs, outside, and toward the café. I could smell the coffee and fried bacon when I walked in. I sat down at a table and a young woman came to take my order. Several other men sat in the café, probably getting something to eat after work. Although they all stared at me, none seemed particularly anxious to talk. When my food came, I asked my waitress if I could hang a sign on the wall about our meetings.

"What kind of meetings?" she asked. I told her that I would explain about the good news of Jesus and how we can be sure to go to heaven.

"We will have meetings all week long," I said. She pointed to a place where several notices were already posted. I thanked her and told her I would return later with a poster. "When does the train from Arkansas arrive?" I asked.

"In about an hour," she answered.

I finished my breakfast, paid, and walked outside. The town was quiet. Even though it was still morning, the summer heat was already stifling. I was beginning to feel weak, so I went back to my room to lie down until Lee's train arrived.

***

It was so good to see Lee again. We took his suitcase to the upstairs room, and I set up the second cot. We talked for a long time. He told me all about the new congregation at Alpena and the excitement of worshiping together. Each man took a turn teaching from the Bible. The older women were teaching the younger women, and all were learning to love each other like Jesus does. The news thrilled my heart.

I told Lee about my family and of my desire to become an American citizen. It had only been nine months since I'd left Alpena, and yet it seemed like years. We talked about the upcoming meetings. I wanted to give many of the same sermons I had given in Alpena, telling the stories of my life and using the "Two Roads" chart. Lee offered to lead singing, give his testimony, and help follow up with

salvations. We talked about the fact that those who would come might include miners and their families, farmers and their families, and American Indians. I wondered if any of them would be able to connect with my life. Whether they did or not wasn't as important as whether they connected with the Holy Spirit. Lee and I prayed for the Lord to do His will in this place.

***

I was thrilled when the first meeting, like the one in Alpena, drew many to the salvation God offers through Jesus' blood. Men, women, and children listened with intense interest. I noticed one young woman who sat in the back. She seemed shy. When the last of the audience left, she slipped quietly out the door with them. She came back the second night, and on the third night a young man came with her. I found out later he was her husband. She came forward to talk with me, and her husband walked out the door.

"I am Sovola London. Could you come to our home for dinner?" she asked. It was a gracious offer and I accepted. I told Lee that I needed to follow through with this couple and asked him to conclude the meeting with prayer.

I climbed into their wagon, having no idea where they were taking me. Their house was in the country a few miles outside of town. It was a simple farmhouse. Lawrence worked in the mine as a loader, but also tried to produce a cash crop on their land. It was a hard life. They had been married only a few months and were still full of hope.

Sovola was interested in hearing more about Jesus, but Lawrence was skeptical. He said he didn't have time for church. Sovola had begged him to come with her after the first night, but he refused. On the second evening, he was plowing in his field and the brilliant sunset appeared to be the fires of hell, so he decided to come with his wife the next night. When I talked about the two roads, he realized he was on the wrong one. He wanted to know more.

Sovola had made a delicious meal, and I enjoyed their company very much. It occurred to me that they were both about the same age as Wallace, younger than Frank. They could be my children. We set up four chairs in their kitchen, one for each of us and one for the Lord, as Freddie and I had done with guests back at home. By the end of the evening, two new souls were added to God's kingdom. Tears of joy flowed, and in heaven the angels rejoiced.

Lawrence took me back into town and left me at the school. I told Lee all about the Londons. He'd had a successful evening too, and many were saved. We continued to teach from the Bible the last two nights, and then Lee packed his things so that he could return home. I wrote Freddie a long letter and told her about Lawrence and Sovola. I wanted to stay with them for another week and teach Lawrence more from the Bible. He was an eager student, and I believed God was going to use him at gospel meetings, too. He needed to be carefully and correctly trained.

It was good to share the scriptures and stories with Lawrence. As it is said, the teacher often learns from the student. Since Lawrence

had to work at the mine during the day, our time was limited to the evenings. I convinced Lawrence to take me to the mine since I had never seen the inside of a working coalmine. Walter Wilson had told me about the deplorable conditions he had seen in the mines in southeast Missouri before he moved to Kansas City. I, too, was shocked to see the filthy, unhealthy, and dangerous environment that Lawrence entered every day. From that moment on, I often prayed for their safety.

It was time to go home, and I was leaving behind a new congregation of believers in Henryetta, led by Lawrence. Lee Grisham was leading the group in Alpena, and the two leaders promised to keep in touch and help each other whenever they could. I invited Lawrence and Sovola to come to Kansas City to meet Freddie and the people at Central Bible Hall. God was doing great things.

On the way back home I felt at peace, and I slept well. I had been gone only two weeks, but at home big changes had been taking place. I was going home to more surprises.

Chapter Twenty-Seven

Double Wedding

The train approached Union Station in Kansas City. Home again. I looked out the window and saw a group of people on the platform. Freddie stood there, always easy to pick out because she's the shortest. I smiled. Bert, Ada, little Maurice, Nettie, George, Paul, Frank, and even Wallace stood with her. I wondered who the two other girls could be. Must be friends of Nettie's, as they didn't look at all familiar to me.

I gathered my things and walked toward the exit, stepped off the train, and gave Freddie a hug and kiss. Then I hugged each of my children. Everyone seemed happy to see me.

Frank said, "Dad, I'd like for you to meet Mabel Hord."

I extended my hand and said, "Hello."

Immediately, Wallace said, "And I would like for you to meet Lois Minton." Again, I extended my hand and said hello.

"Well, let's go home and eat. We have a lot to talk about," said Freddie, trying to encourage all of us to leave the conversation until later when we'd be in a more comfortable setting.

Bert and Ada drove their car with George, Paul, and Lois in the back seat. Wallace rode his motorcycle, and Frank, Mabel, and Nettie rode in the front seat of Frank's car, leaving Freddie and me alone in the back seat. It felt good to know home was only a few minutes away. I could almost taste the good meal I knew waited for us there. The young people in the front chattered away, while Freddie and I quietly enjoyed being together.

When we got home, everyone jumped out of the vehicles and the clamor of setting the dinner table for twelve began. The aromas of Freddie's cooking didn't disappoint. We all sat down, prayed, and began to pass the bowls of food. Everyone wanted to hear about my trip, and I was happy to tell story after story. Our guests seemed to enjoy them just as much as our own family.

Freddie and Nettie cleared the dishes and served dessert. Finally, I told them about Lawrence and Sovola London. I reported that they were young, and yet were establishing their marriage on a Godly foundation.

"Speaking of godly young couples, Dad, Wallace and I are hoping to add two to our family," Frank said. I know my face showed my shock.

"Okay," I said slowly. Both the girls were looking at me with big smiles on their faces. I looked at Freddie and she nodded. Nettie took the conversation from there.

"Papa, we thought we could have a double wedding right here at home." It surprised me that Nettie was comfortable planning a wedding for her brothers when she had hoped she would be planning her own only a year earlier. But I was happy that she had such a wonderful attitude. She continued, "If we have it on September 26, we can celebrate yours and Mama's thirty-fourth anniversary, too. Mabel suggested we have the pastor of her church do the ceremony so you can just enjoy the day with Mama." They certainly have planned it all out, I thought.

"Well, we certainly do have a lot to talk about," I said. "Could you give me a day or two to take all of this in?" I looked at Mabel and Lois.

In unison, they said, "Of course, Mr. Capp."

"Thank you," I said.

Nettie and the girls asked to be excused. They went up to Nettie's room, and giddy laughter oozed out from under the door. I told Frank and Wallace to meet me in my study in a few minutes. They

left the table and I helped Freddie clear the dessert dishes and followed her into the kitchen.

"Why didn't you tell me about this?" I asked my wife. I wasn't really angry, just overwhelmed.

She took my face in her hands and said, "Papa, this is not the kind of news you'd want to hear in a letter, is it?" Of course she was right. I needed to hear this face to face. She hugged me and said, "Go talk to your sons."

As I walked down the hall to my study, I prayed. I didn't want to crush anyone's hearts, but there was so much to find out first before I could give my approval. I didn't want to damage my relationship with Frank and Wallace like I had with Nettie. This was going to be touchy. I trusted Frank, but this was happening quickly and I wanted to be cautious. Wallace, of course, had given us reason to question his judgment. Would this girl be good for him? I went into the study.

***

After weeks of talking with my sons and spending time with their intended spouses, I had become more comfortable with their choices. Mabel had a good job at a bank. She was from Clinton, Missouri, and had met Frank through business contacts. She was a nice girl, and she went to Western Highlands Presbyterian Church regularly with girlfriends. Marie, her sister, would be her maid of honor. Our

first impression of her parents was that they were pleasant and friendly.

Lois was quiet and yet polite and respectful. She was from a small town, Hodge, Missouri, along the rail line near Lexington, Missouri. Wallace had met her at the hospitality house for the railroad in Hodge. Lois helped served at the hospitality house. Her family lived in Hodge, and her father was a farmer. He had given the couple a few acres of land, and Wallace planned to grow crops. I had seen from Freddie's family and from Lawrence London how hard the work of farming could be. I wasn't sure Wallace could handle it, but I wanted to believe it would be good for him. And he was in love, so he believed he could do anything.

The wedding plans were on. Nettie and Freddie spent a lot of time working on invitations, decorations, and refreshments. There would be a large cake for the wedding couples and a smaller cake decorated with anniversary sentiments for Freddie and me. Nettie would be Lois's maid of honor, so she and Marie Hord worked on dresses for each of them and on both of the bride's dresses. Paul and George would be attendants for their brothers.

The week of the wedding, goldenrod and fall flowers gave our house the festive look that Nettie and Freddie were well known for. Rev. George Sutton came, and we had a pleasant talk about the ceremony, the scriptures he would use, and then about his church and my travels. We gathered everyone together and had a rehearsal. We hoped Maurice, who was just learning to walk, would be able to hold a

pillow with the rings secured with ribbons. Ada tried to guide him down the aisle between the chairs we had set up. We knew it might be too much to ask from the toddler, but it was fun, anyway.

The day finally came. Nettie had stayed overnight at Mabel's apartment to help the brides with last minute details. Also, with the girls away, Frank and Wallace would not see them in their dresses before the wedding. Both brides' parents arrived in the afternoon, and they helped Freddie set up the punch bowl and refreshments. The cakes were placed on a beautifully decorated table. I tried to stay out of the way and help the boys stay calm. Our guests started arriving at seven-thirty. C. J. Baker and his family were among the first to arrive. It was so nice to have good friends attending this important occasion. Walter Wilson and Marion came a short time later. By eight o'clock, all the guests were seated and it was time to start. Music filled the house as the pianist from Central Bible Hall played on our upright piano. The girls had arrived and were at the back door with their fathers. Freddie and I took a seat in the front row. Rev. Sutton, Frank, and Wallace entered the front door and took their places. Maurice, with Ada's help, performed his ring bearer duties perfectly. The brides made their entrance. Everything went as planned, and Freddie and I could not hold in our tears of joy.

***

The party went late into the night, and everyone marveled at the fruit of our efforts. The brides and grooms were going to spend their wedding nights in a hotel that Frank had arranged, so after the

cake and punch were served and the seventy-five guests were greeted, they were ready to leave. Nettie and Marie had prepared little bags of rice, and we showered the newlyweds with it in our front yard as they sprinted to Frank's car. George and Paul had decorated the car and tied tin cans to the back bumper. The kids were on their way to their new lives. Frank and Mabel planned on living in a house in Kansas City, Kansas, and Wallace and Lois were going to the farm the next day. Our guests began to leave. The Hords would stay overnight in Mabel's apartment and go back to Clinton in the morning. The Mintons had to drive back to Hodge. They said they must get home because of farm duties. Freddie, Nettie, and I were exhausted, but with George and Paul's help we quickly cleaned up and went to bed. The flowers, streamers, and left over cake would remind us of this happy time for days.

Chapter Twenty-Eight

Wallace

The weeks after the wedding took our sons down two very different paths. Frank and Mabel were able to take a honeymoon, and when they returned, Frank and his friends made their plans for the Christmas Eve Santa visits. Freddie and I wondered how Mabel would feel about being alone on Christmas Eve, but she supported her husband and didn't seem to mind. Of course, she knew she could spend the evening with us. Nettie and Freddie always made our home a delightful place for everyone, especially on Christmas.

Wallace and Lois went to the farm the day after their wedding. He had quit his job at the railroad. Lois's family was in the midst of harvest season, and there was a lot of work to be done. I did not know what agreements or expectations Wallace's new in-laws had, but I was afraid the "romance" of working the soil would lose its charm with my

son. I just didn't know how soon. We didn't see Wallace and Lois very often, but I knew that they kept busy. Sometimes the couple offered to bring the crops to the city, and then they'd visit with us a little before going back to Hodge. They stayed in the country for Thanksgiving, but we hoped they would be at our house on Christmas Eve.

December 24, 1916 finally arrived, and all our children and spouses were present, but Frank was late due to his alter-ego appearances. God was at work, I knew, but in my heart I sensed something would turn our lives upside down again. I asked God to give us His peace no matter what happened. We ended the evening with singing, as usual, praising God together for the wonderful gift of His Son.

***

A few weeks later, Freddie and I were startled by an unexpected visit by Frank. It was cold outside, but no snow lay on the ground. He had an uncomfortable and unusual panic about him as he said, "Mama, Papa, there has been an accident. I've come to take you to the hospital." We rushed to get our coats and followed him out the door.

On the way to the hospital, Frank explained that Wallace and Lois had wrecked his motorcycle on the Inter-city viaduct. They had been coming to visit us. They hit a patch of ice and crashed into the bridge's concrete abutment. Freddie and I immediately started to pray.

Our son and his wife were hurt, and we knew that only our Great Physician could heal them.

When we arrived at the hospital, we were first directed to the room where Wallace was being treated. His face was so broken that it was hard to recognize him. He was in shock, but other than his face, he didn't seem to have any other major injuries. Freddie took him in her arms and held him. I asked the doctor about Lois.

"I'm afraid she is not as fortunate," the doctor said. "She is unconscious, and we don't know the full extent of her injuries yet." I couldn't imagine how her parents would cope with this. To the best of my knowledge, they did not have a relationship with the Lord. I prayed for healing and for opportunities to comfort them.

Wallace wanted to see his wife, but I wasn't sure if that was a good idea. He insisted, so with the doctor's permission, we went into her room with him. His own injuries made it hard for him to see, but what he did see was enough to make him collapse in agony. We lifted him and returned him to his room.

"Son, put your trust in the Lord. He alone can help." Wallace cried, and we joined him.

After a few days, Wallace's face was black from bruises, but the doctor said it was going to heal. He had several broken bones in his face, but there was no way to set them. It was difficult for him to eat or talk. We kept a notepad by his bed so he could write what he wanted to

say. He went to Lois's room every day to hold her hand, but could only manage it for short periods of time.

Lois's family had come as quickly as they could, and after spending time with their daughter and the doctors, her brothers came to Wallace's room, understandably angry and upset at him. They screamed curses and lunged at him. Freddie and I, along with the hospital staff, had to restrain them. I offered to pray with them in the hallway, but they would have nothing to do with me or my God. I had to leave them to grieve alone, but I continued to pray for them.

A couple of weeks later we took Wallace home with us. Lois had regained consciousness, but had severe internal injuries and remained at the hospital. Wallace didn't want to come to our house, but he really had nowhere else to go. Nettie spent a lot of time with her brother, and he trusted her to tell him about Lois since her parents didn't allow him to visit her.

Walter Wilson and C. J. Baker also visited Lois regularly and kept us updated, even after the doctors sent her home. Her condition improved a little, but she still suffered a lot of pain. She didn't ask to see Wallace, but she told Walter that she forgave her husband.

By March, Wallace was well enough to work again. He wanted to join the Army, but he did not pass the physical exam. Instead, he applied to work again with the Union Pacific railroad. The clerk job he left in September had been filled, but there was an opening for a clerk in Cheyenne, Wyoming. The farther the better, he felt. Freddie and I

were not happy that he was going so far away, but we understood that he felt helpless in going forward in his marriage and with his life in Kansas City. Even more disturbing to us was that he was not turning to the Lord.

***

Wallace wrote to his mother and sister throughout the spring, telling about the beautiful country. The cool mountain air seemed to renew his energy. I think he was afraid to ask about Lois. In July, Nettie went on a trip to see a friend in Seattle and stopped on the way to see how Wallace was doing. I was so thankful he was able to have a close relationship with his sister. She had a tender heart, and I knew she would be able to comfort him.

Sadly, on August 20, Lois went home to be with the Lord. During a visit with Walter, she had given her life to Jesus. She never really recovered from her injuries and quietly slipped into eternity. C.J. and Walter went to Hodge and gave a beautiful message at the funeral. Walter sang, "Safe in the Arms of Jesus." Her family never let go of their anger toward us and toward God.

In September, Wallace enlisted in the U.S. Army in Cheyenne. The war was raging in Europe, and an influenza epidemic was spreading through the Army bases, but Wallace didn't care. The railroad would have a job for him when his commitment to our country was fulfilled.

Paul enlisted in the Navy, so now two of my sons were seriously planning to serve in defense of the United States.

Christmas 1917 was especially meaningful. All of our children were home except Wallace. He was scheduled to start boot camp at Ft. Lewis, Washington, after the first of the year. He didn't say it, but I knew he was still hurting from all that had happened in the past year. I wanted to tell him I loved him, but he was so far away.

Paul was home from the Navy and he brought a friend. Esther Mauvin had been writing to him for several months after Jeanette gave her his address. Her bubbly personality brought new fun and excitement to our house. Late in the evening Frank arrived, still dressed in his Santa suit. We ended with our carol singing tradition and with prayer. I thanked the Lord for our family and asked that He would watch over Wallace and keep him safe. Somehow I knew that the next year would bring even more changes and challenges.

Wallace 1944

Chapter Twenty-Nine

Becoming a Citizen

I had stopped attending my night classes when I went to Oklahoma. The wedding and the accident delayed my history and government studies even longer. But becoming a U.S. citizen became a priority to me again. It seemed the whole country was focused on the war efforts and our family was no exception. Professor Morgan welcomed me back. With his help, I filed the necessary papers with the Department of Immigration and Naturalization declaring my intent to become a citizen. I understood it would take time, but I felt God's urging to give my word of loyalty to the country that had been the only home I could remember.

As I studied, I learned about the faith in God that was the driving force in the lives of most of the Founding Fathers. The documents were filled with language that spoke of the God of the

Bible, His mercy, and His guidance. The Lord showed me over and over how this country was special because of its reliance on God. My sons were fighting in military units that represented the United States, and I was proud. I hoped my family in Germany was safe too, but it had been so long since I'd seen them, and I had no idea how this war was affecting them.

I was asked to preach for two weeks in Belleville, Kansas in March, so I took those weeks off from my studies, and many people were led to the Lord. However, something else happened at home during that time that took both Freddie and me by surprise.

Paul came home for a short leave and was scheduled to sail from San Diego after that. Esther had been writing to him daily. Freddie, of course, was happy to see our son, but what happened next put another stressful schism in our family. After attending Central Bible Hall with his mother and sister on Sunday, Paul left Monday without telling Freddie his plans. He and Esther took the train to Edwardsville. There, Bert and Ada and a judge from Leavenworth met them. Paul and Esther were married and came back that evening. Nettie was the first to find out, and she started planning a celebration at our house. When I came home Freddie was very upset, but she didn't want Paul to leave with unresolved conflict at home. She helped Nettie with the preparations and forgave Paul for not telling her. At the party, Paul and Esther announced that they would be going to San Diego by train for their honeymoon. In two weeks Paul would board his ship and Esther would move into a small apartment in San Diego

with a girlfriend. I believed that was a good idea, and we could get used to their marriage before they returned to Kansas City. For Freddie, forgiving Esther was a process that couldn't be rushed.

It was important to me to keep in touch with the men I had led to salvation. Lawrence London and Lee Grisham began working with the Plymouth Brethren, and I received letters from them regularly. They asked many difficult questions and I spent hours of research each week to make sure my answers were correct. I also had several requests each month to preach. Sometimes requests came from Central Bible Hall and other times from farther away, but I tried to stay fairly close to home. Often, if Lawrence or Lee asked, I went to their meetings to preach one or two messages. It was so uplifting to me to see these young men doing the Lord's work.

In June, Wallace wrote to let us know that he was going to Europe. His unit would go to France, but he didn't know any details. The only thing I knew to do was to pray. With two of my sons involved in this war, I didn't know where they were or whether they were safe. It was a test of my faith. If they died, I couldn't be sure of their salvation. So I let go and put my trust in the Lord. Freddie was the Army's contact person for Wallace, and she received an allotment check. It was the due payment for his service, but the money was no comfort for a mother unsure of her son's fate. Freddie and I joined others to pray for our children. Nettie and many of her friends assembled and sent care packages to the soldiers.

Christmas was especially sad again. We tried to be joyful, but it was difficult when our hearts were so heavy. If our loved ones were not injured by war, would they escape the clutches of the dreaded influenza? I thought that God had perhaps spared Wallace from the disease by his rejection to join the Army in Kansas. Ft. Riley was hit the hardest. However, we also heard of the gas attacks at Argonne, France. Was Wallace there? Where was Paul? Peace on earth …would it ever be? Nevertheless, we sang praises to the newborn King and put our trust in Him.

***

The year 1919 brought glimmers of hope. Bert and Ada presented us with our second grandchild, Robert Standish Capp. I loved babies. They brought new life and a reminder that God had not forgotten us.

Wallace returned to Wyoming in April, and the next month he was discharged from the Army. He secured a job with the Union Pacific in Kansas City again, so he came back home to live. Freddie and I were so happy to see him. He had seen and experienced a lot of things during the war, and seemed more serious and more mature than before. He was quiet and didn't want to talk, but he worked hard and sometimes went to parties or picnics with Nettie, George, and their friends.

At one of the meetings where I helped Lawrence, he told me that he and Sovola were expecting their first child. I knew they had

been waiting a long time for this child, and Freddie was thrilled when I told her. They planned to name this child Frank, in honor of my firstborn son.

***

The years were taking their toll on my strength and energy. I talked to Walter Wilson again, and he believed that insulin was going to be a big break through for treating diabetes. Meanwhile, he recommended that I rest more and avoid rich foods. I wondered how I would be able to resist Freddie's cooking. It was hard, but I tried. I knew the Lord was my real strength, and He would provide all I needed.

Wallace, Nettie, and George lived with us, and all were working and contributing to our finances. We purchased a house at 67 S. Seventeenth, and it didn't take long for Freddie to make it our home. I spent my days studying both the Bible and American history. Freddie had more time to work with the women from Central Bible Hall. They provided food and clothes for the needy and taught Bible classes to women and children. Whenever a person needed aid, Freddie was the first to respond. Her love seemed to know no boundaries.

By the summer of 1921, Professor Morgan thought I was ready to take the exam for naturalization. There were 105 men from nearly every country in the world at the examination. The questions were difficult, but Professor Morgan had prepared us well, and sixty-seven

of us passed the requirements. On July 6 I entered the Wyandotte county district court room with the two men I had chosen to be my witnesses—Frederick Nail, a salesman and a member of Central Bible Hall, and my dear friend Walter Wilson, who had encouraged me from the beginning of this adventure. My wife, all of my children and their spouses, and my grandchildren were present. Freddie beamed with pride and love as I walked in with the other men. We lifted our right hands and repeated the oath of allegiance together: "...so help me God," I said. Tears ran down my face. I realized finally that I was truly an American.

A huge throng of people gathered around me as we left the courtroom. At home, Nettie and Freddie had outdone themselves with the patriotic decorations and food. Just two days earlier we had celebrated the nation's birthday with fireworks, but today we celebrated my citizenship. We prayed and thanked the Lord for this occasion and that both my sons had come home safely.

Chapter Thirty

Jesus, the Anarchist

Because I had become a citizen, I had the right to vote and be active in government. However, in my Bible study, the Lord was showing me more about His kingdom. For believers, this world is just a temporary home. The kingdoms of this world, including the United States, will not be permanent, so we should store up our treasures in heaven where they count for eternity. The souls of men, women, and children are more valuable than all the silver and gold the world can offer. This was the basis for a new message, "The Jewish Anarchist," that I preached at my meetings. It was clear to me that Jesus was the ultimate anarchist, because His kingdom is not of this world. He broke all the religious laws, and yet His law of love fulfilled the spirit of those laws. He ate with sinners and healed on the Sabbath, but He always did His Father's will. My heart was filled with joy when I experienced, even deeper, the freedom His love and forgiveness had

secured for a wretch like me. I wanted to share that freedom with everyone.

Paul and Esther returned to Kansas City after the war, and Esther became a great help to me. She kept my study in order and wrote some letters for me. I was glad that Freddie had let go of any hostility toward her because of the elopement. Shortly after they returned to Kansas City, Paul and Esther's first son was born. They named him William. Esther brought Bill with her to our house, and Freddie played with him for a couple of hours on the days that Esther worked in my study.

I spoke regularly at Central Bible Hall and took an occasional trip to either Belleville or Arkansas. I was obviously weaker due to my health, but I learned to slow down a little. I made trips to San Antonio, Texas, and to New Mexico. Everywhere I went people listened and were saved. In October of 1922, Alvin Miller, a pillar at the Belleville congregation, suddenly fell ill and died during a series of meetings. I was called to fill in for him and complete the week. It was decided that although his death brought sadness, he would have wanted the meetings to continue. After his funeral, I returned home. In December, Freddie and Frank joined me as I returned to Belleville for three days at the Belleville Believers Bible Conference. Frank's music was a beautiful addition to the meetings. On Saturday night Walter Wilson joined us, and he gave a message on Sunday morning.

Our family Christmases were even more enjoyable with the addition of our grandsons. Bert and Ada had Maurice and Bob, and

Paul and Esther had Bill and Don. When Santa arrived with the ringing of bells and a loud "Ho-Ho-Ho," the little ones' eyes widened and laughter filled our house. It was fun, but I never let the birth of the Savior get lost in the celebration.

Wallace was more settled than he had ever been, and in December 1923, he married a girl from the Clinton, Missouri area. Alverda Belle Bartlett was a fun-loving girl he had met through Nettie. They were married in Clinton, near where her family lived. When I found out that the Bartletts were Jehovah's Witnesses, it was very disturbing to me, because I knew that the Witnesses held to some false teachings. I decided to keep quiet about my fears, though, because Belle made Wallace happy. I knew our relationship would not survive a rift like the one with Jeanette. Belle did not seem to agree with her parents' religion, and she came to Central Bible Hall. I knew she was hearing truth there, and I believed she had a true relationship with the Savior. I did not know how her parents felt about us. Wallace still worked for Union Pacific in the Argentine district, and Belle worked at the telegraph office.

Shortly after Christmas that year, George married a girl named Ida Polson, so all my children except Nettie were settled into their own homes.

With her job and the organizations she belonged to, Nettie traveled to far away places in the United States, as well as abroad. She came home with wonderful trinkets and stories. Even at home, Nettie was always busy with her friends, and she seemed happy.

Walter Wilson continued to advise me about my health. The use of insulin injections for diabetes seemed like a great breakthrough, so we tried it. I had trouble with my right arm, which Walter thought could be the result of a mild stroke, but I could still travel and speak. I planned to do so until the Lord called me home.

Wallace and Belle started their family. Richard was born in 1925, and two years later, Charles arrived.

Freddie and I celebrated our fiftieth wedding anniversary in September of 1932. The years had flown by so quickly. Her love for me was only exceeded by the love of our Lord. She was so good to me and I knew that I was blessed beyond anything I could have imagined. Our children planned and arranged a wonderful party. Friends came from long distances to help us celebrate. I thought Freddie was going to faint when her brother Louis Bludorn walked through the door. Nettie had arranged for him to come, and tears of joy flowed for a long time. The day was exhausting for both of us, but after all our guests left and Louis was settled in our guestroom, we held hands and prayed. I loved Freddie so much.

***

About a year later, I knew that my time on earth was coming to an end. I was no longer able to travel, and my eyesight was failing. I visited with people and wrote letters with Freddie's or Esther's help. Walter came regularly to check on me, but one cold January day in 1934, the Lord called me home. I joined Carrie, Leon, and Edward in eternal

worship of our Lord Jesus Christ. It is our hope that you will join us when your life on earth comes to an end.

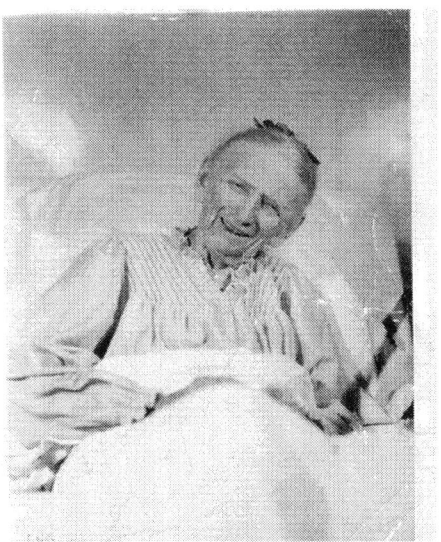

Freddie at 94

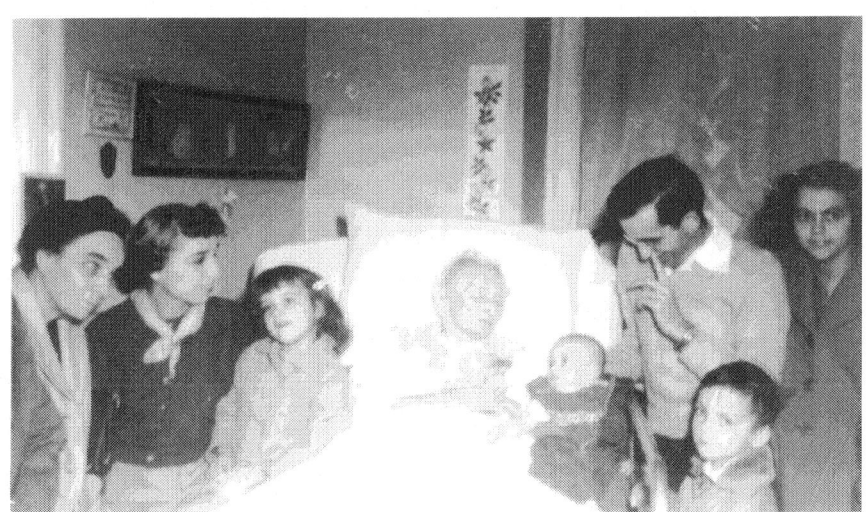

Left to Right: Belle, Connie, Anita (author at 5), Frederica, Leslie (baby), Charles, Michael Ernest, Lucy

Epilogue

Freddie lived for more than twenty years after Michael's death. She continued the Lord's work through her ministry to the needy. Jeanette lived with her mother and cared for her until Freddie fell and broke a hip. Even then, while in a nursing home, Freddie's warm smile greeted all her visitors. On Freddie's one-hundredth birthday, Jeanette planned the last party for her mother—a celebration of her life. I was almost five years old, and I can remember my great-grandmother as a very happy person. Just one month later, February 2, 1955, Freddie went home to be with her husband, her children, and the Lord.

> O Lord, You have been good,
> You have been faithful to all generations.
>
> For by Your hand, we have been fed,
> And by Your Spirit, we have been led.
>
> O Lord, You have been good,
> You have been faithful to all generations.
>
> ~Twila Paris

Appendix

The Two Roads chart by Caleb Baker

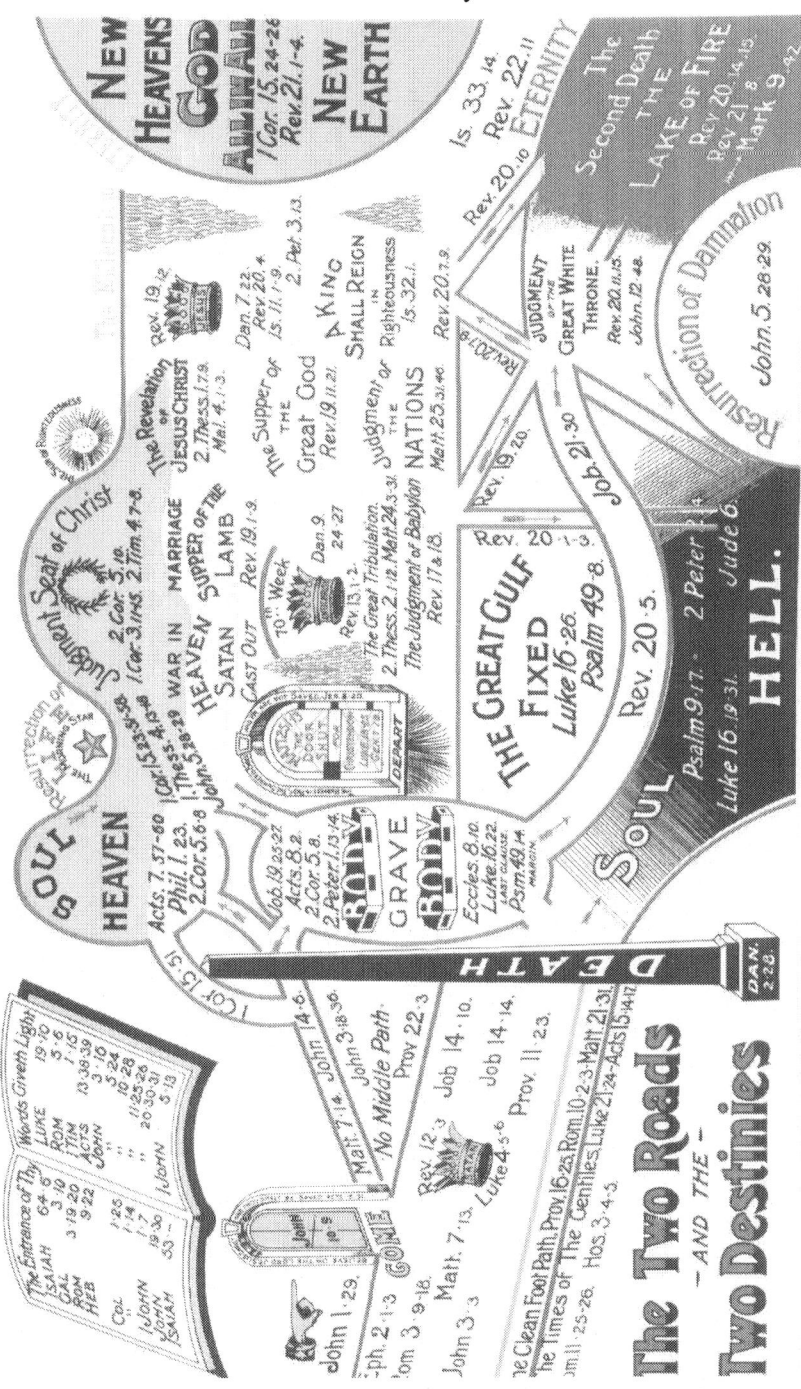